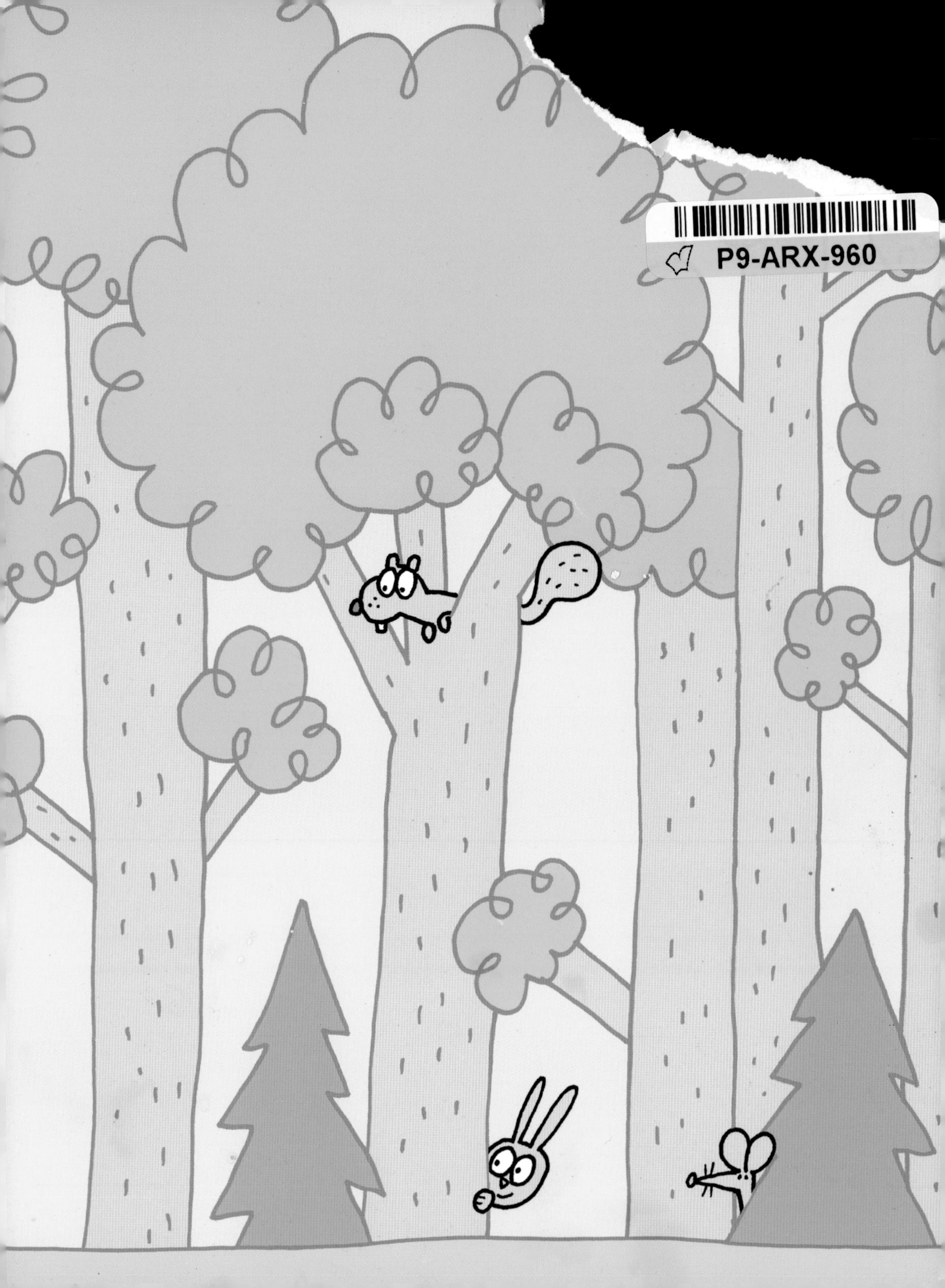

I Really Want a Bigger Piece!
Text copyright © 2022 Harriet Ziefert
Illustrations copyright © 2022 Travis Foster

Published in 2022 by Red Comet Press

All rights reserved. No part of this book may be used
or reproduced in any manner whatsoever without
written permission except in the case of brief
quotations embodied in critical articles and reviews.

Library of Congress Control Number: 2021946360

ISBN (HB): 978-1-63655-019-0
ISBN (EBOOK): 978-1-63655-027-5

21 22 23 24 25 TLF 10 9 8 7 6 5 4 3 2 1

First Edition
Manufactured in China

RED ●
COMET
PRESS

Redcometpress.com

MIX
Paper from
responsible sources
FSC® C104723
FSC
www.fsc.org

A REALLY BIRD STORY

Harriet Ziefert

Illustrations by Travis Foster

I Really Want a Bigger Piece!

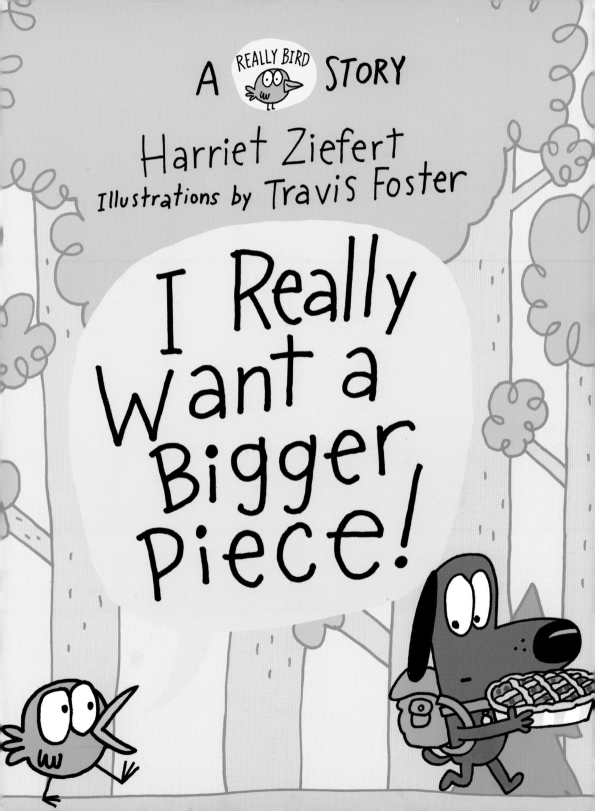

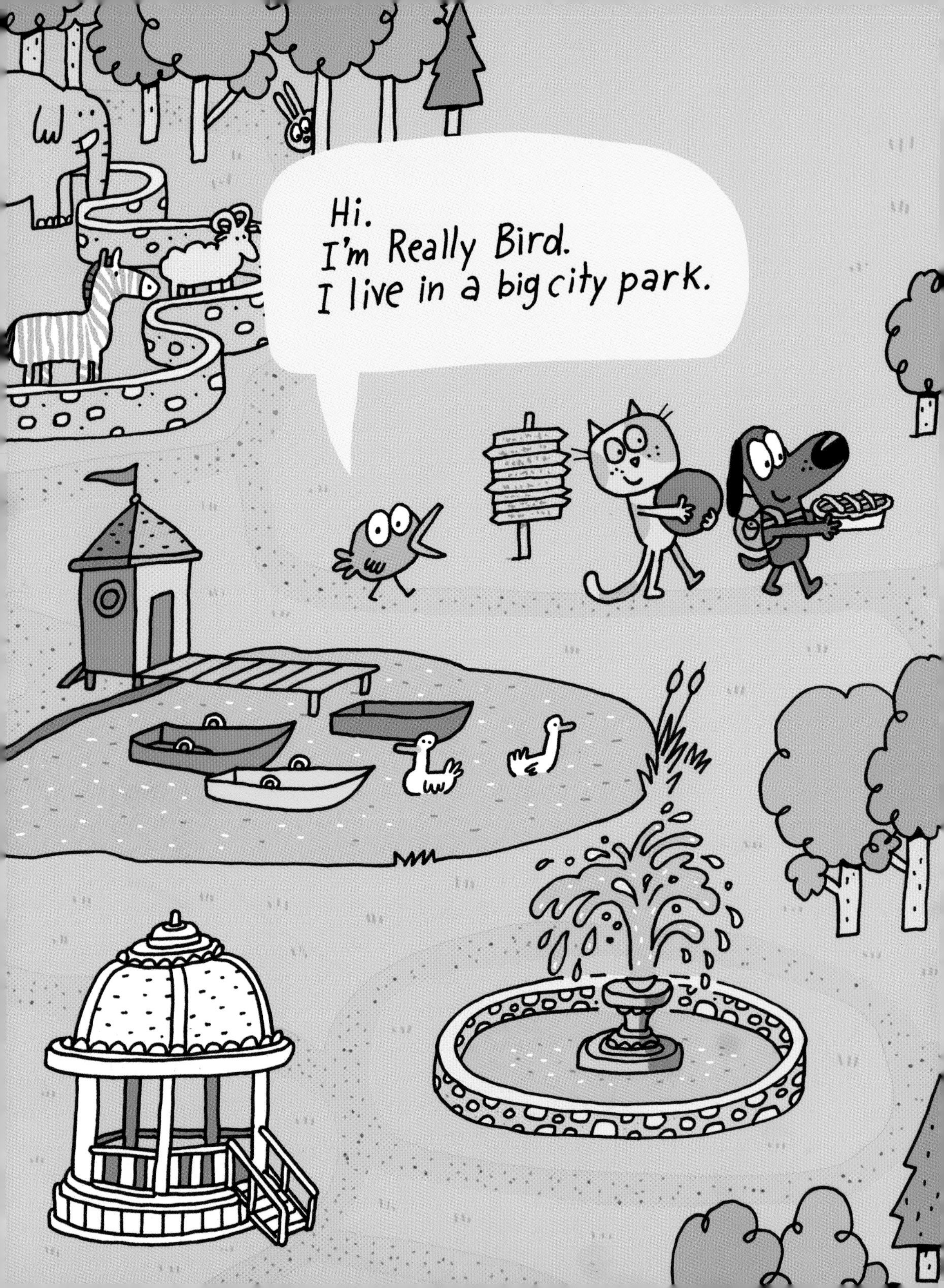
Hi.
I'm Really Bird.
I live in a big city park.

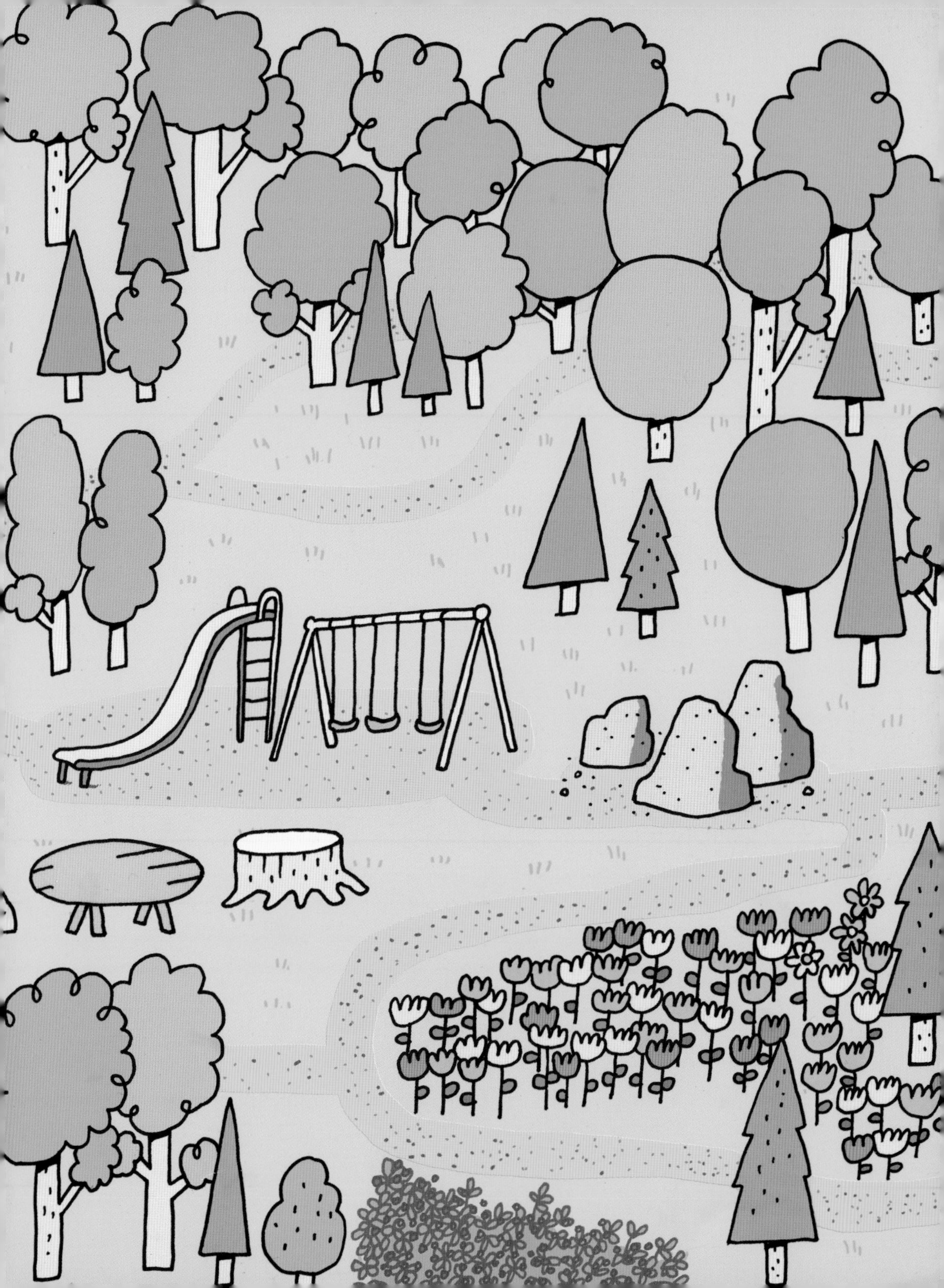

They call me Really Bird because when I'm happy, or sad, or thirsty, or scared, I'm REALLY happy, or REALLY scared... Or REALLY thirsty! Get it?
Today I REALLY want a bigger piece!
WOODS
ROCKS
← ZOO
← BOATHOUSE
← FOUNTAINS
← GAZEBO
GARDENS →
WALKING PATH

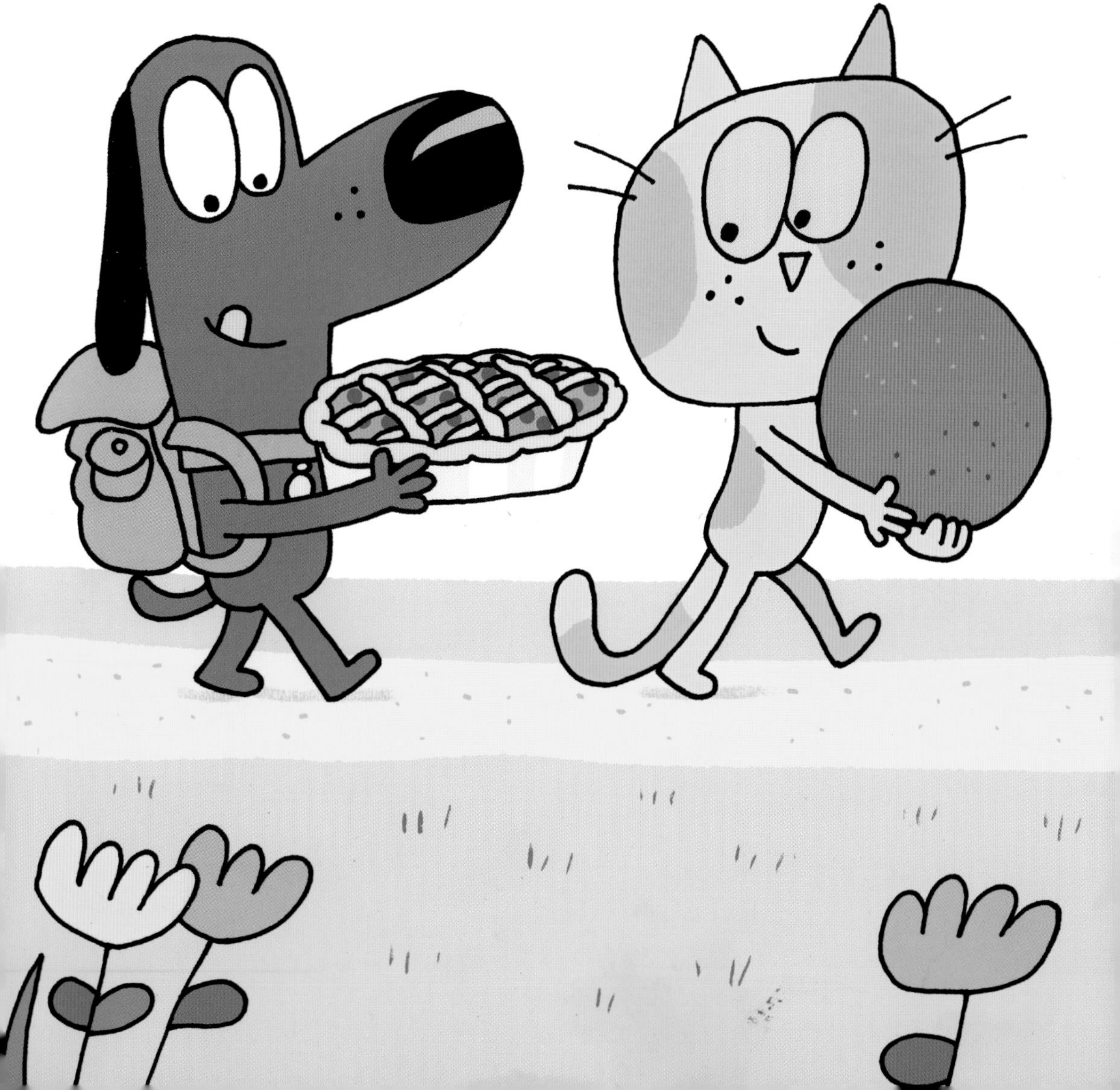

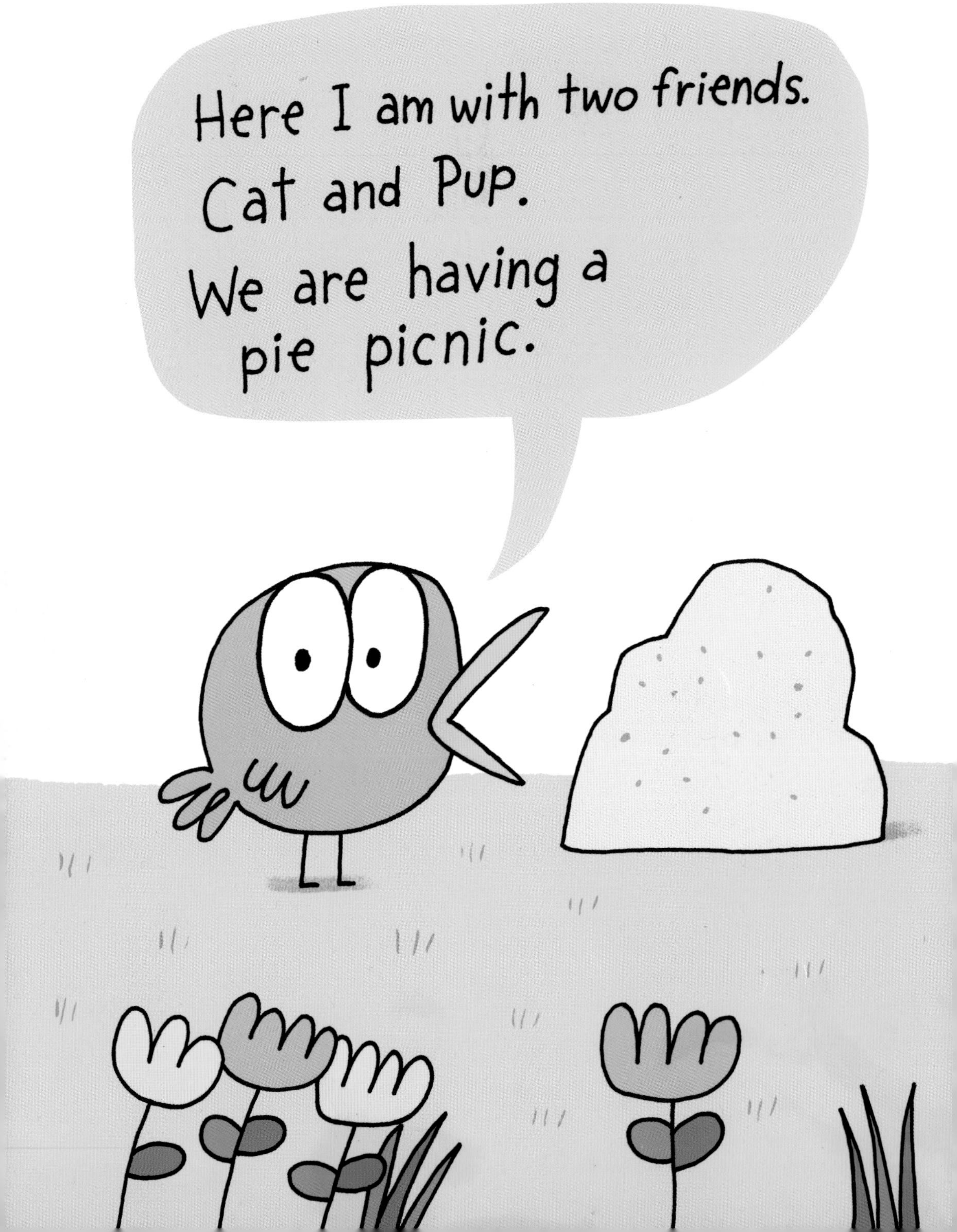
Here I am with two friends. Cat and Pup. We are having a pie picnic.

A yummy blueberry pie picnic!
A homemade, just baked, yummy blueberry pie picnic!

Now we are washing up. First Cat, then Pup, then me! I wait my turn.
I'm SO hungry! I really need to eat!

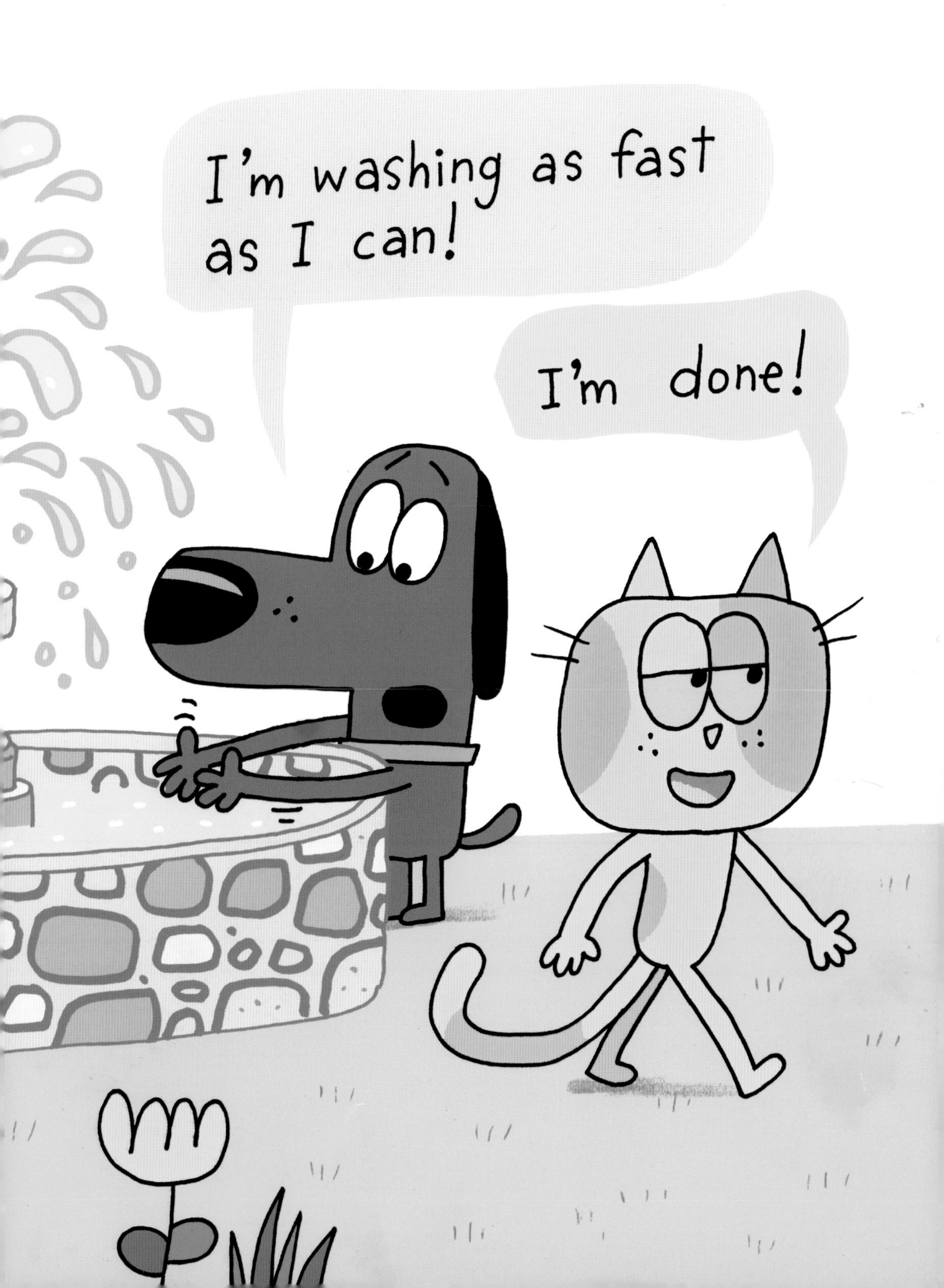
I'm washing as fast as I can!
I'm done!

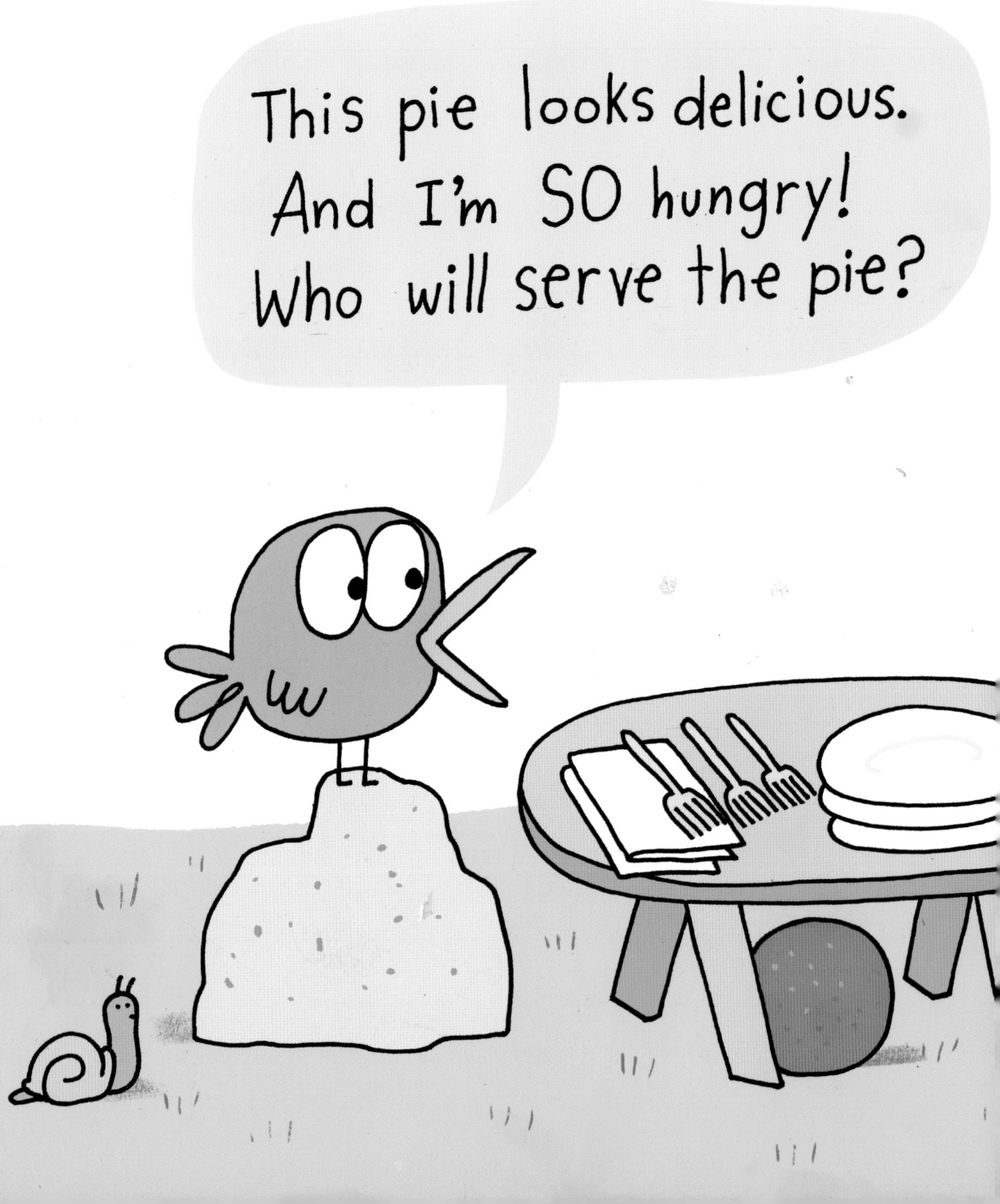
This pie looks delicious. And I'm SO hungry! Who will serve the pie?

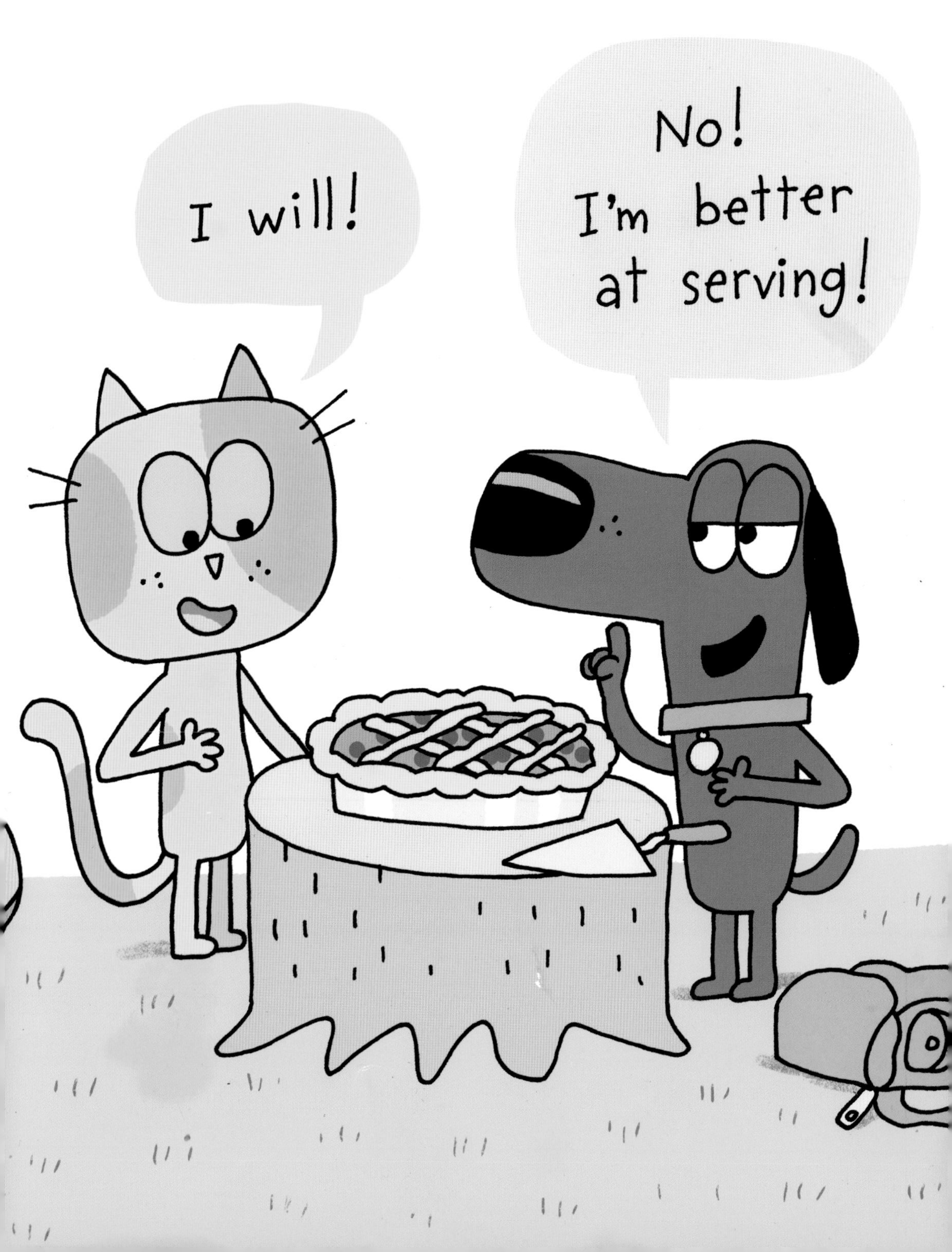
I will!
No! I'm better at serving!

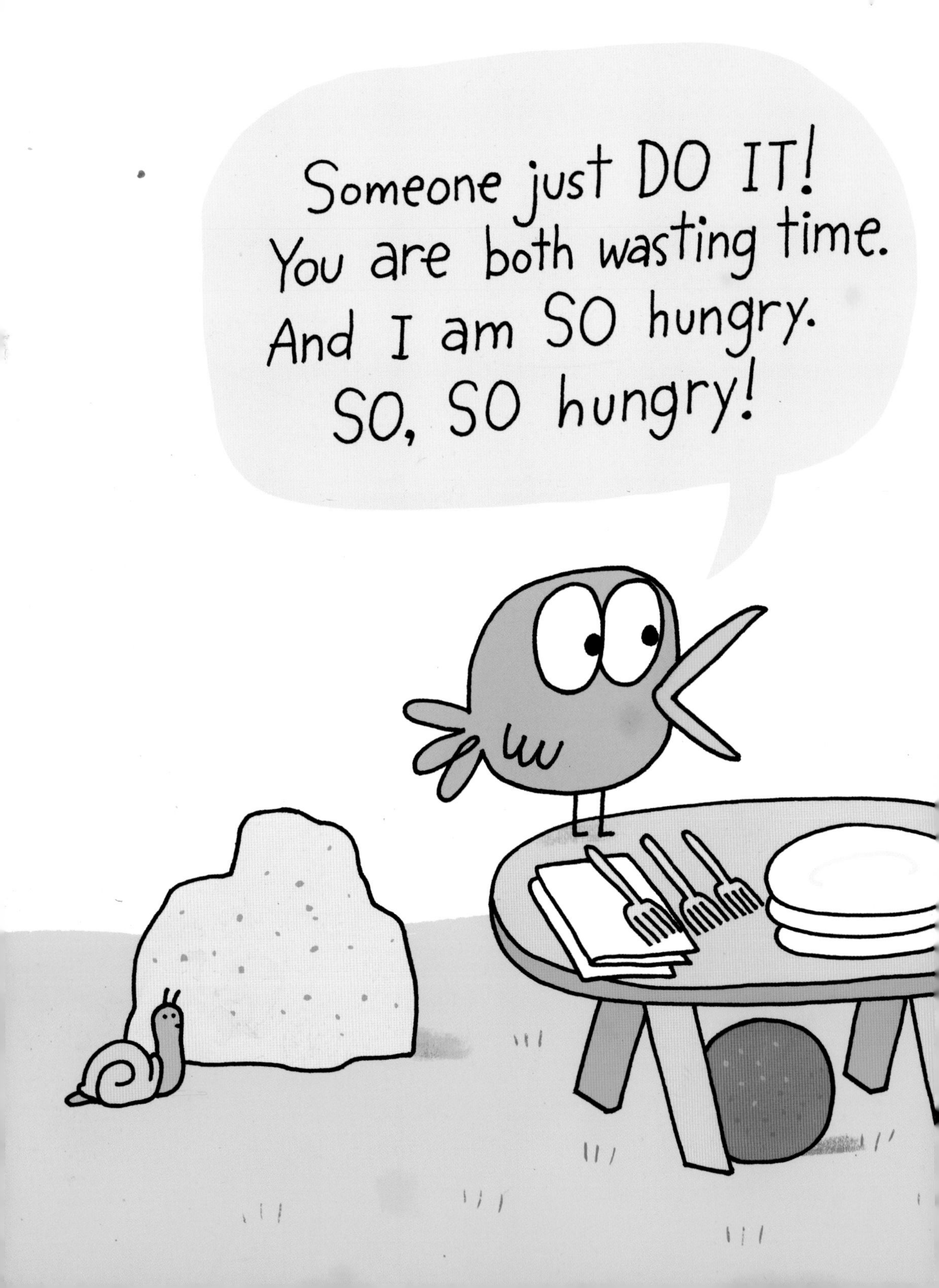
Someone just DO IT!
You are both wasting time.
And I am SO hungry.
SO, SO hungry!

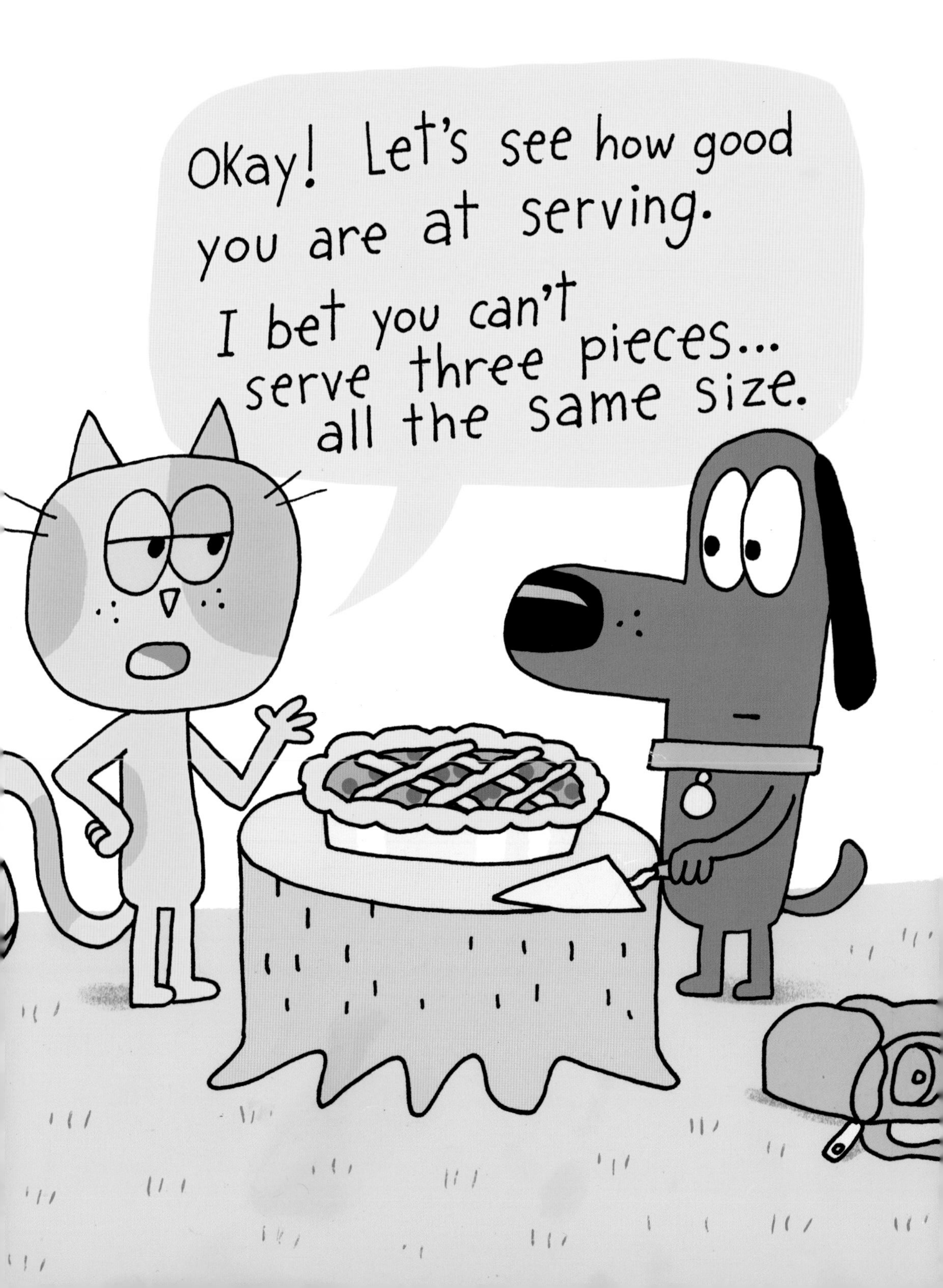
OKay! Let's see how good you are at serving. I bet you can't serve three pieces... all the same size.

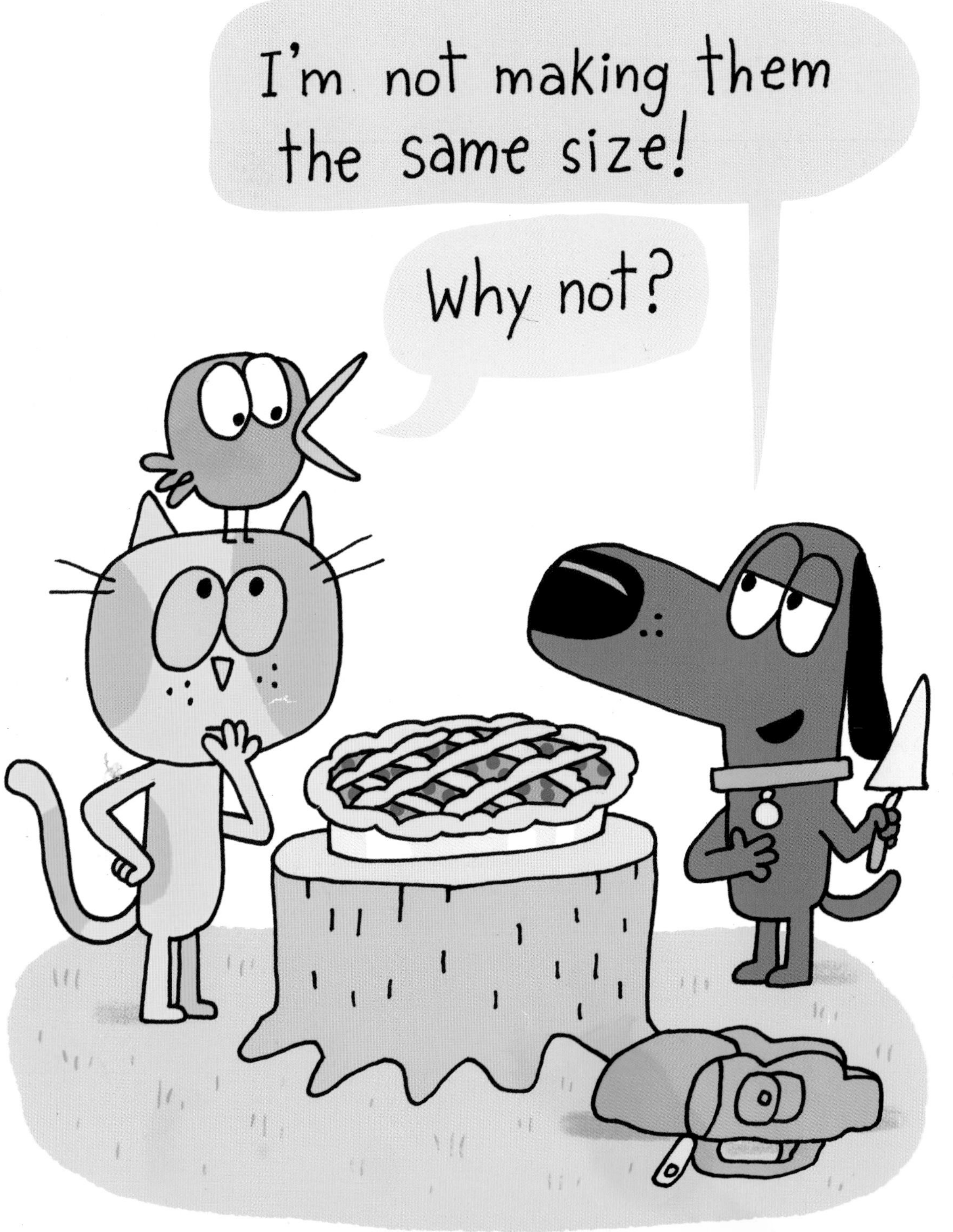
I'm not making them the same size!
Why not?

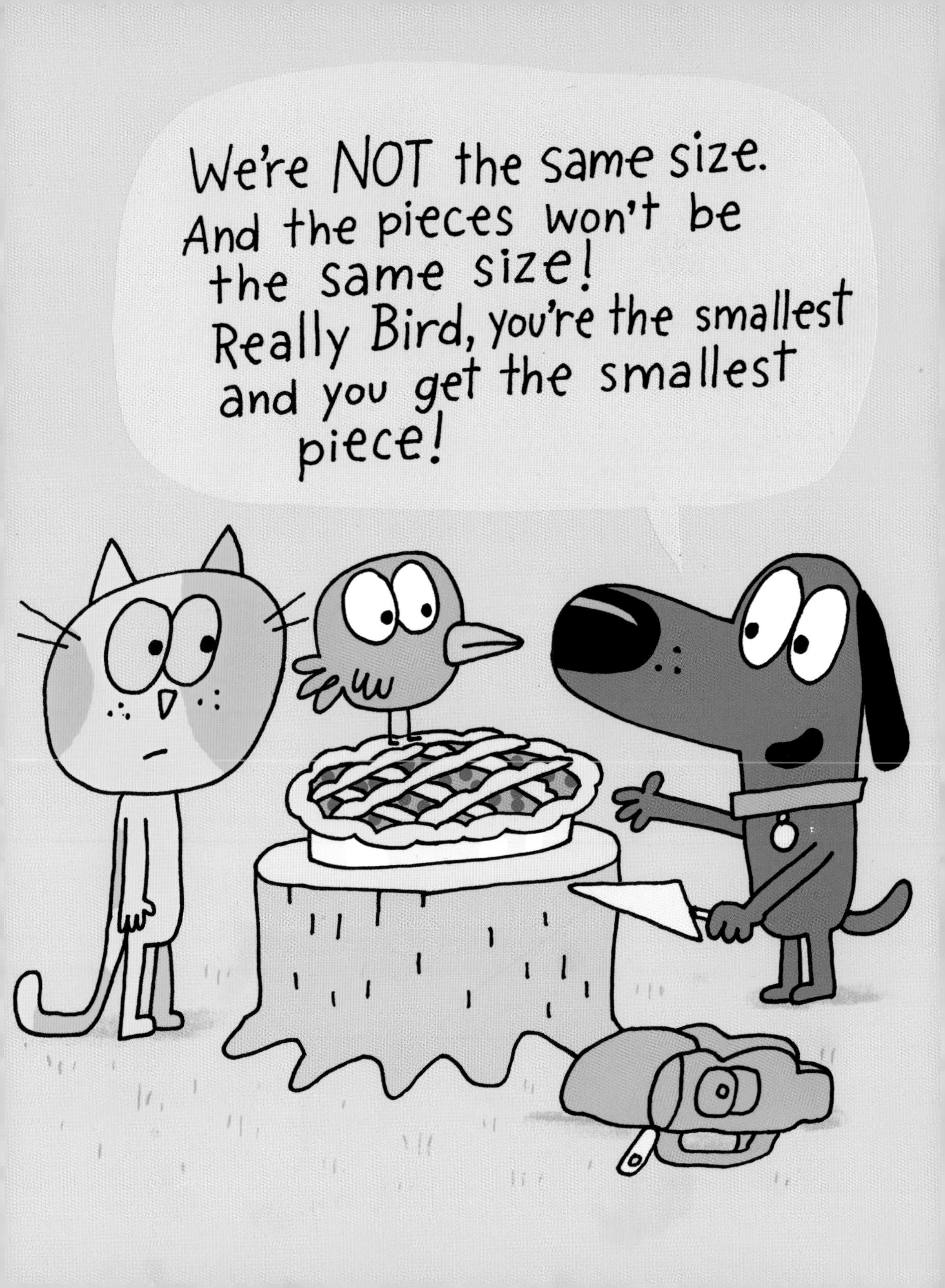
We're NOT the same size. And the pieces won't be the same size! Really Bird, you're the smallest and you get the smallest piece!

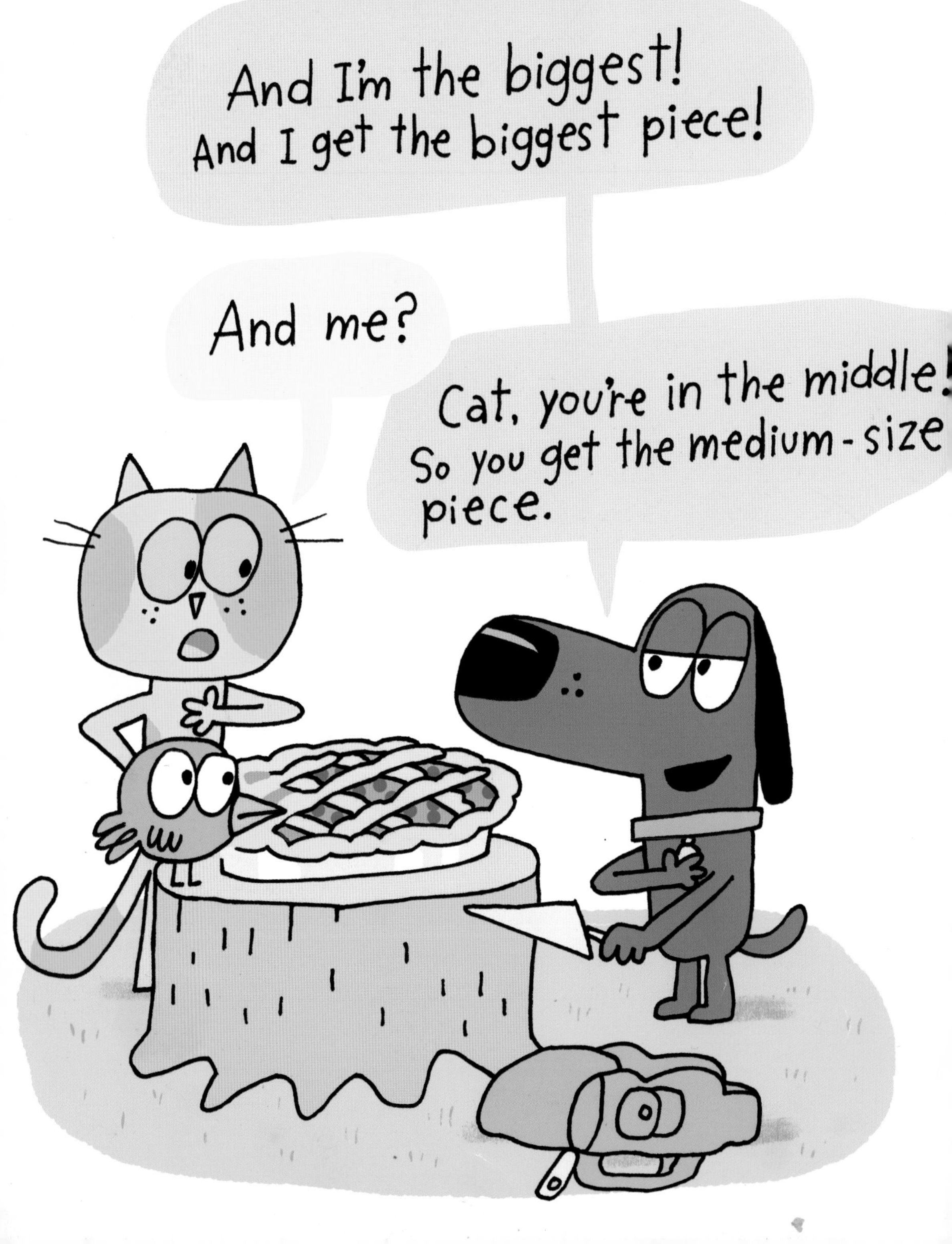
And I'm the biggest! And I get the biggest piece!
And me?
Cat, you're in the middle! So you get the medium-size piece.

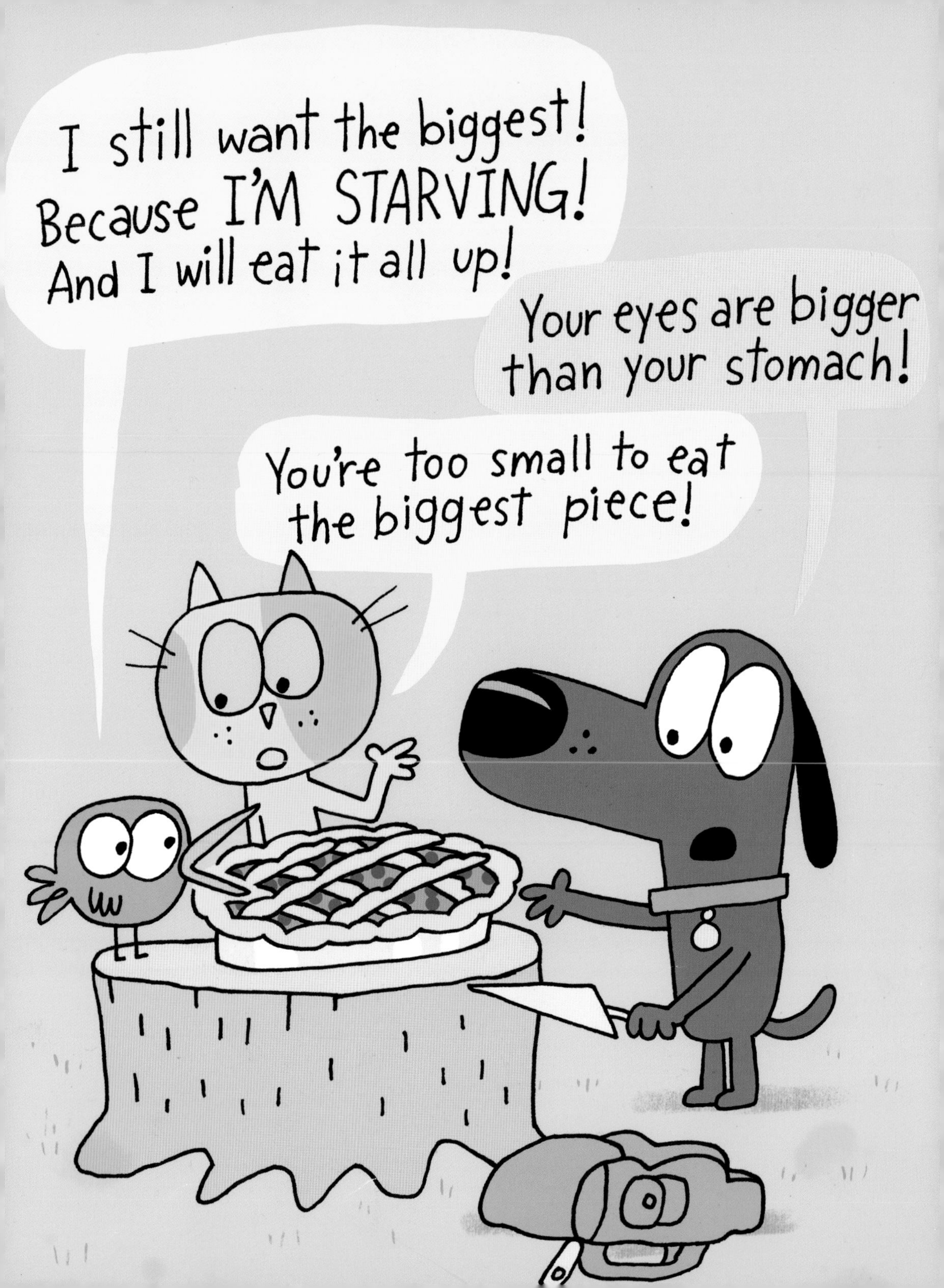
I still want the biggest! Because I'M STARVING! And I will eat it all up!
Your eyes are bigger than your stomach!
You're too small to eat the biggest piece!

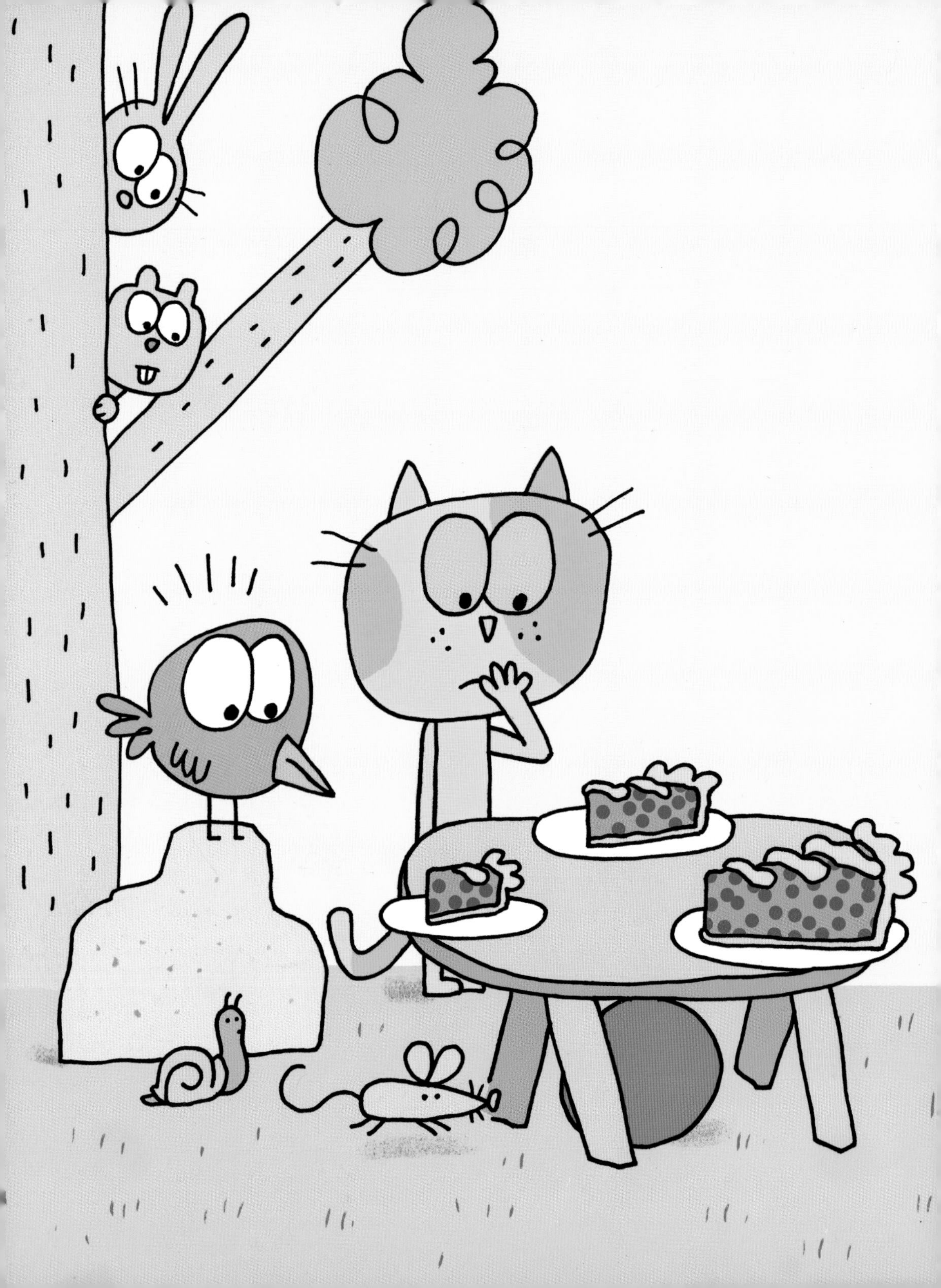

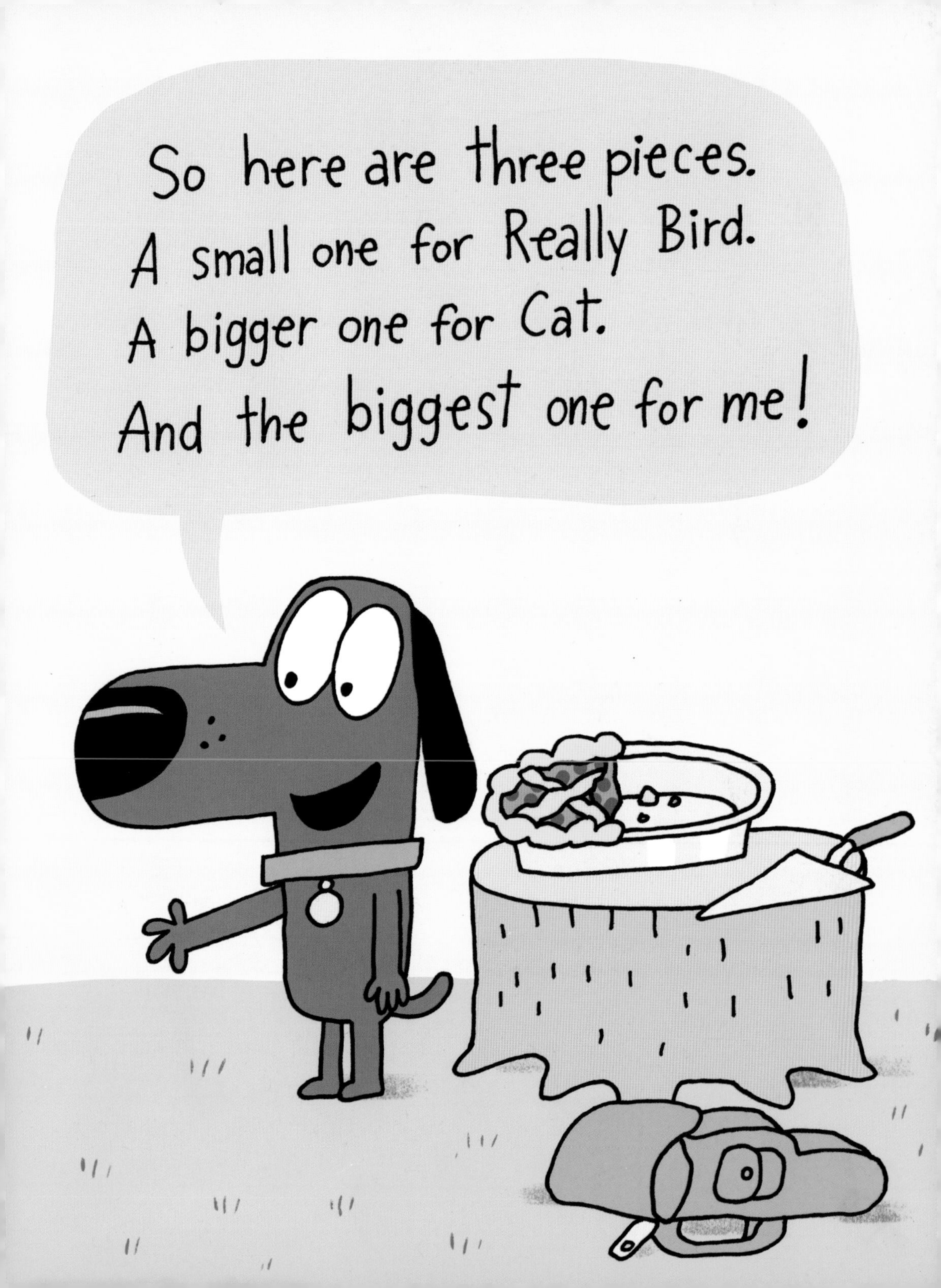
So here are three pieces. A small one for Really Bird. A bigger one for Cat. And the biggest one for me!

My piece is messy! Blueberries are falling out! And some crust is missing!
My piece is too small!

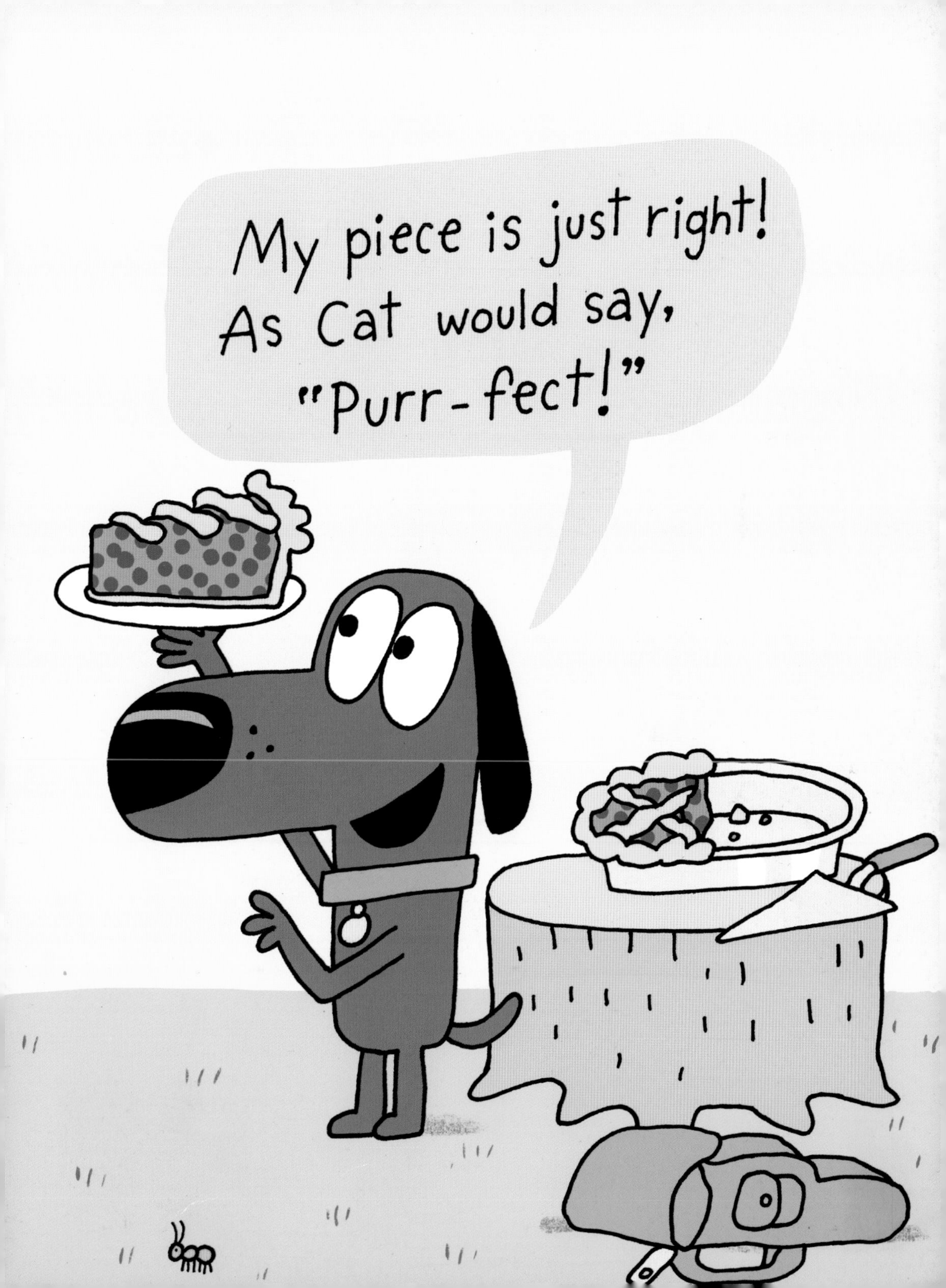
My piece is just right! As Cat would say, "Purr-fect!"

Here we are... wasting time arguing about whose piece is better

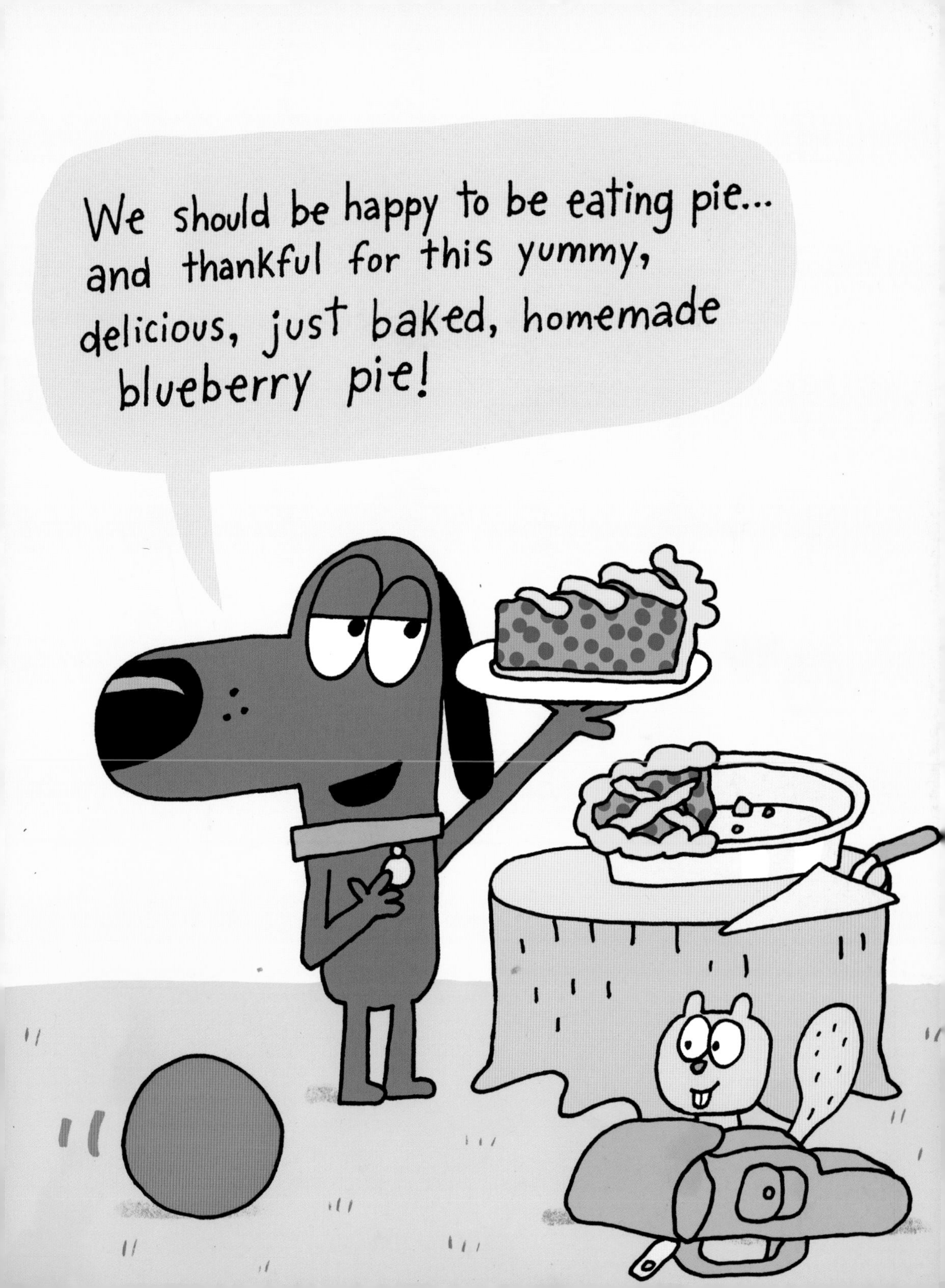
We should be happy to be eating pie... and thankful for this yummy, delicious, just baked, homemade blueberry pie!

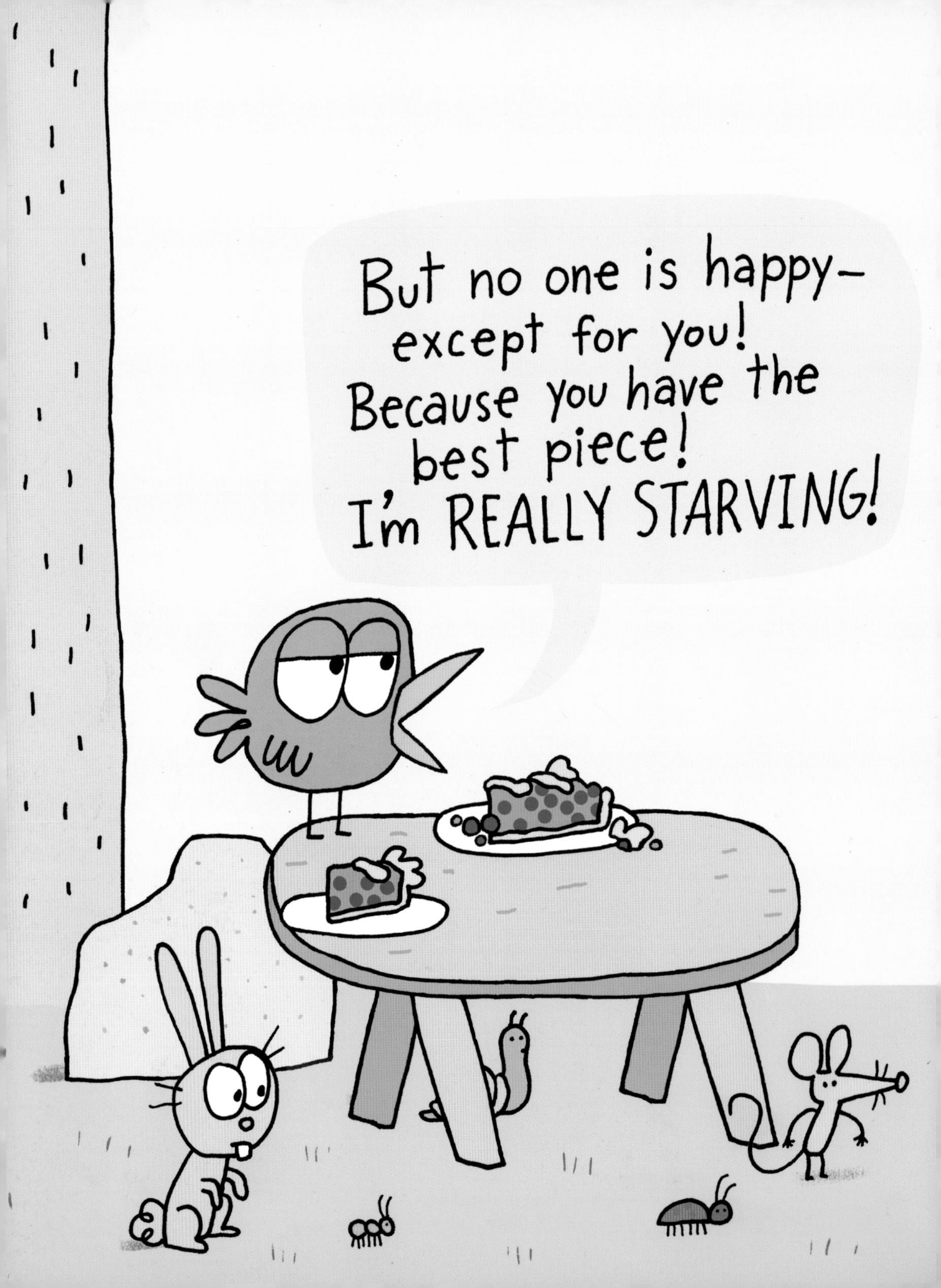
But no one is happy—
except for you!
Because you have the
best piece!
I'm REALLY STARVING!

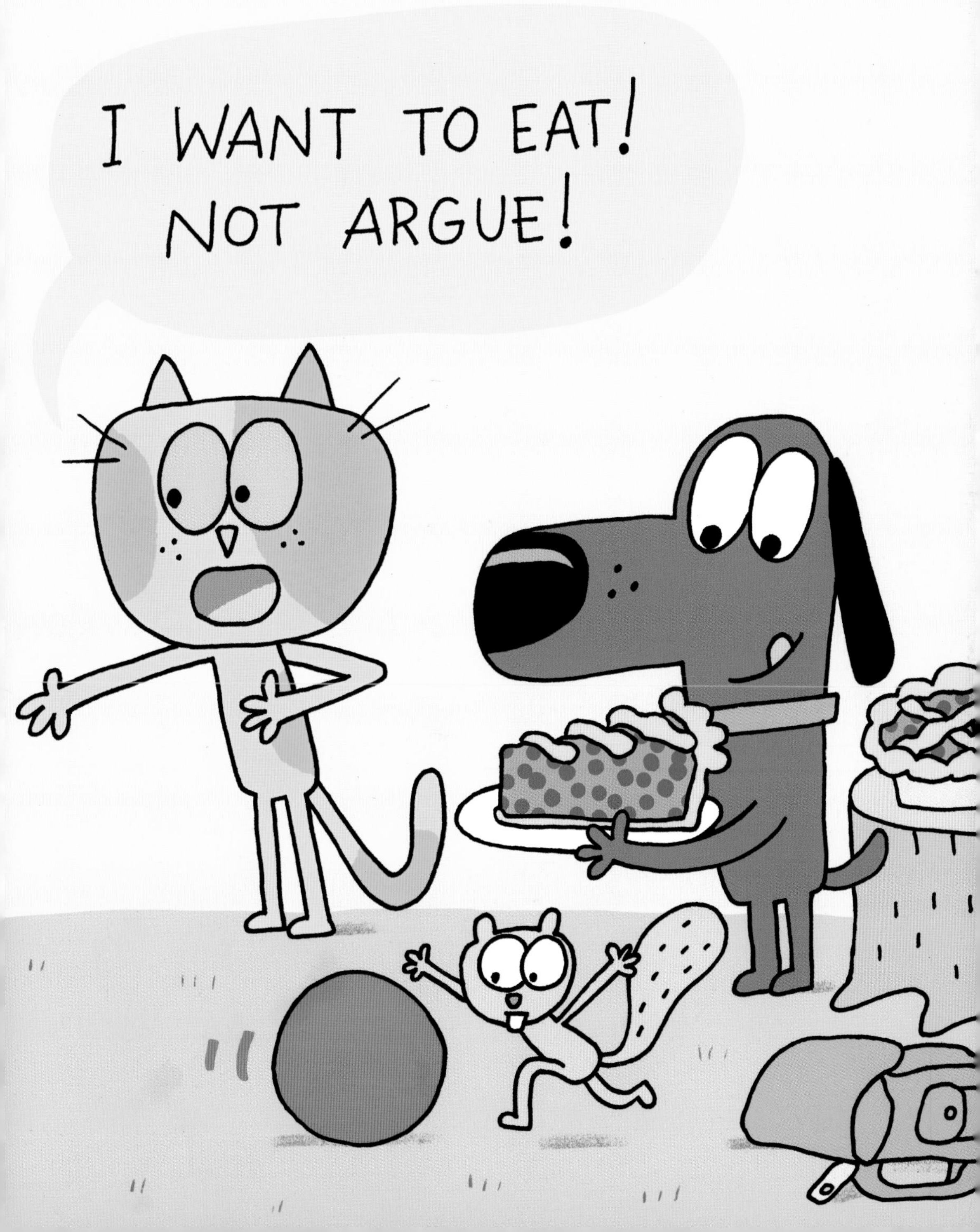
I WANT TO EAT! NOT ARGUE!

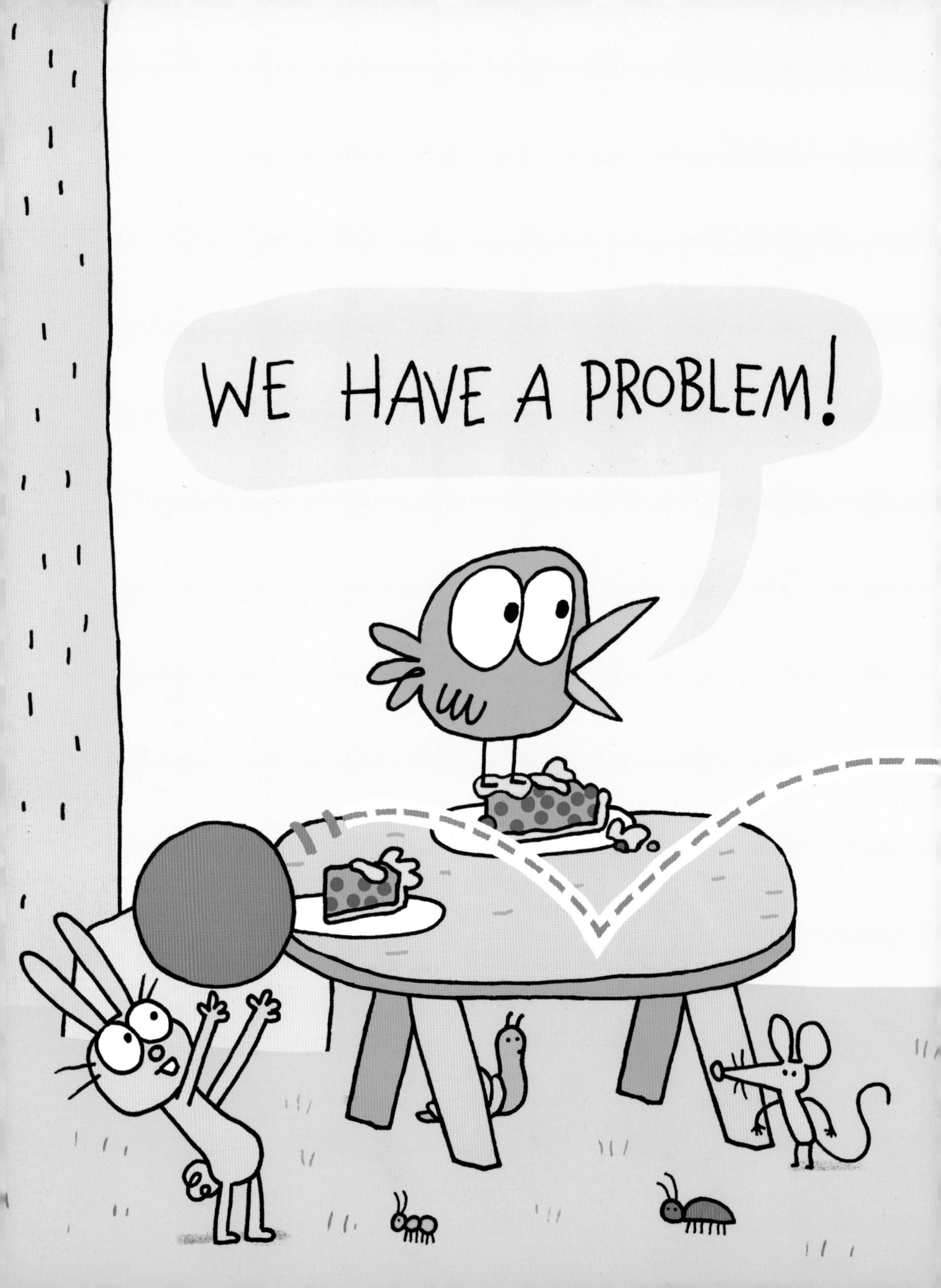
WE HAVE A PROBLEM!

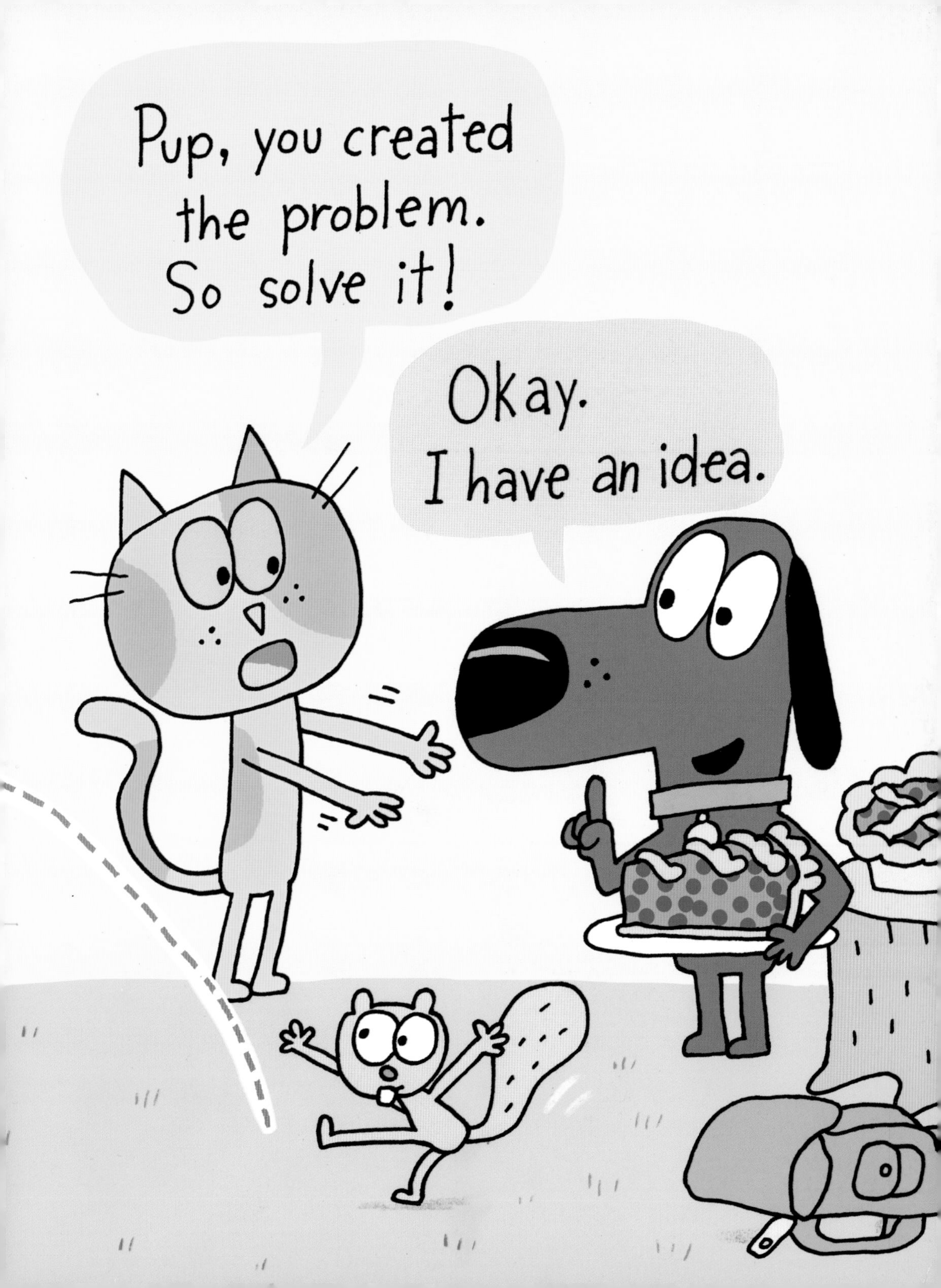
Pup, you created the problem. So solve it!
Okay. I have an idea.

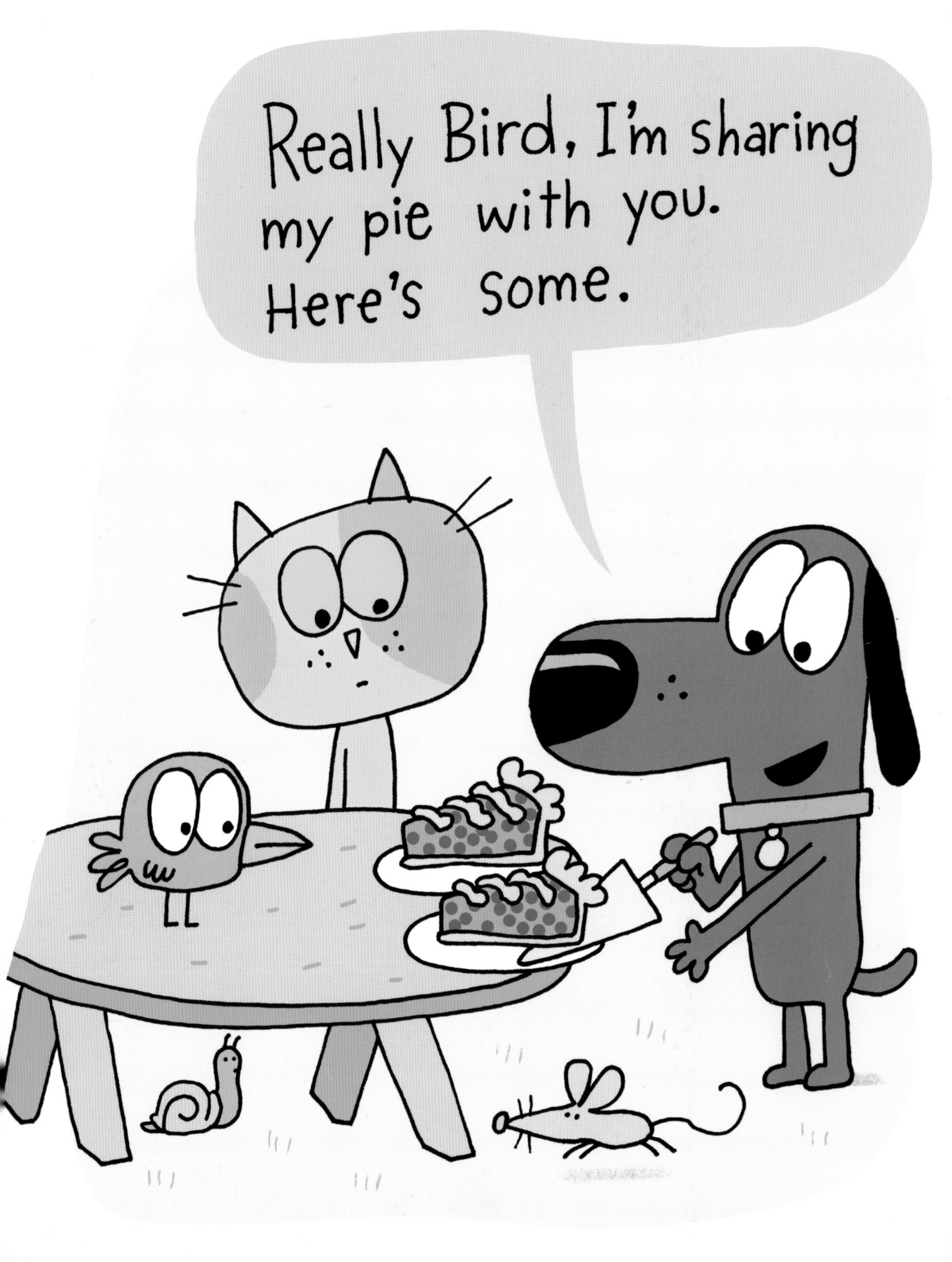
Really Bird, I'm sharing my pie with you. Here's some.

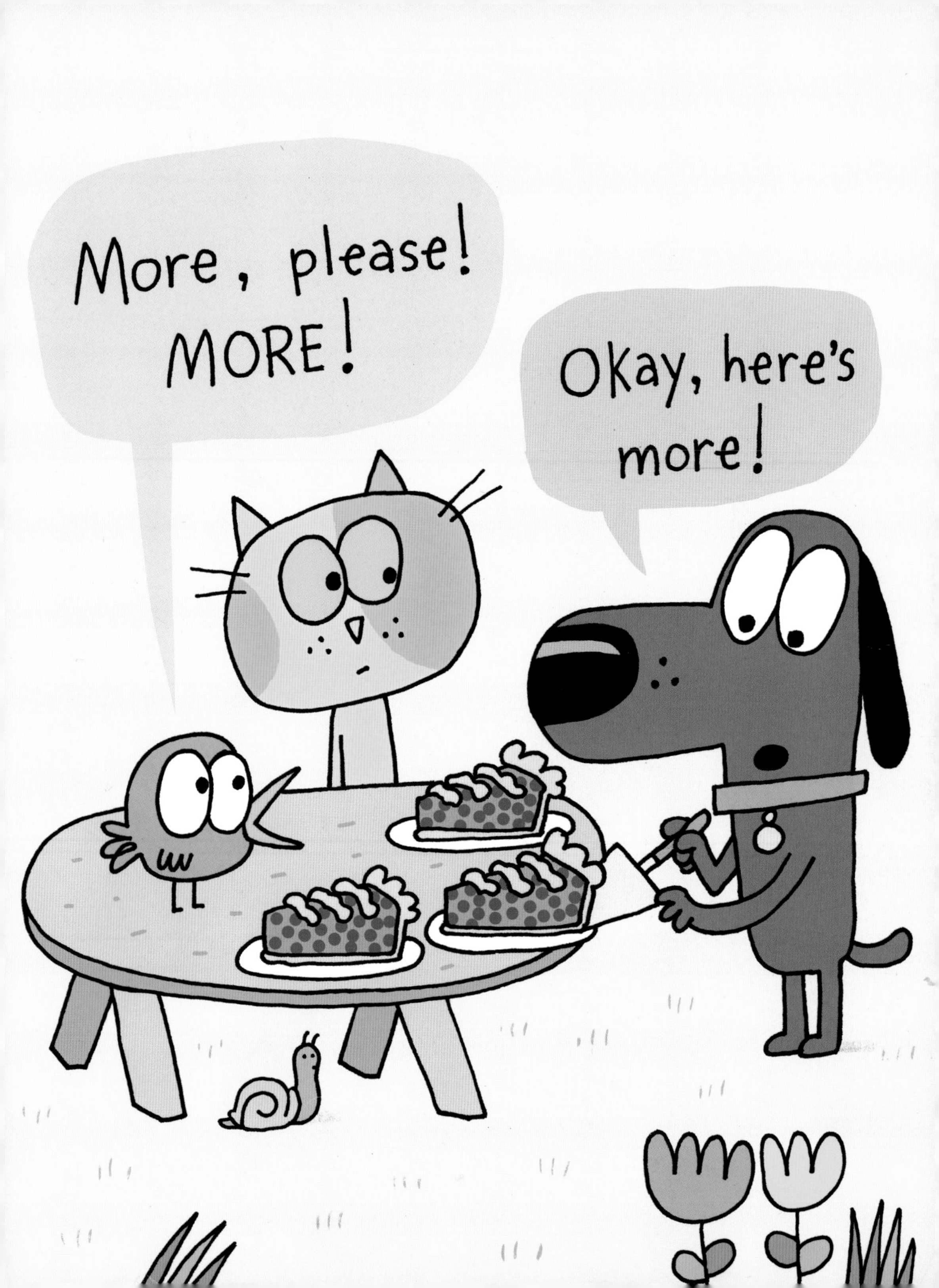
More, please! MORE!
Okay, here's more!

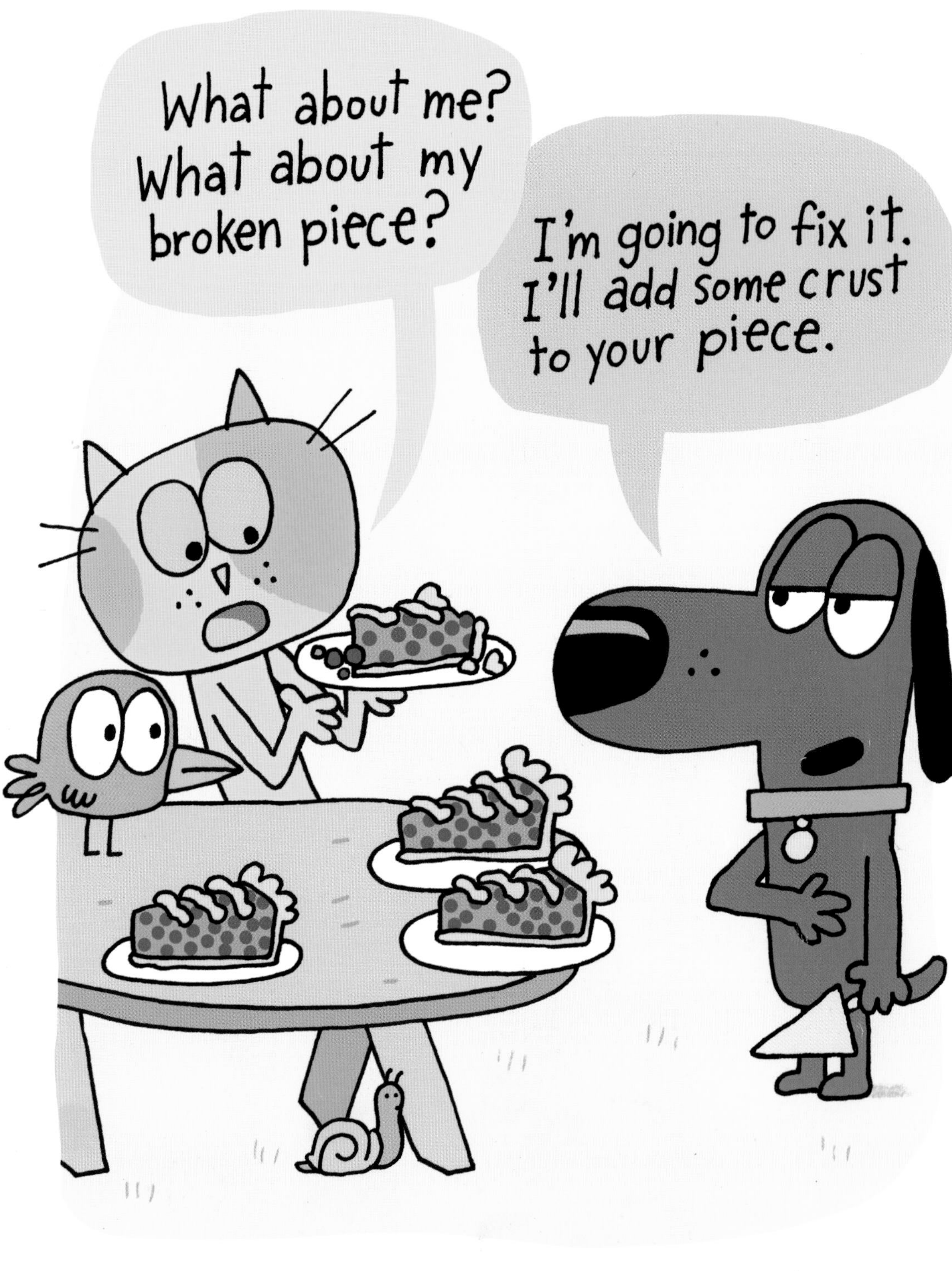
What about me? What about my broken piece?
I'm going to fix it. I'll add some crust to your piece.

Here it is! I fixed it!
It's almost perfect! You can hardly tell where the crust was broken.

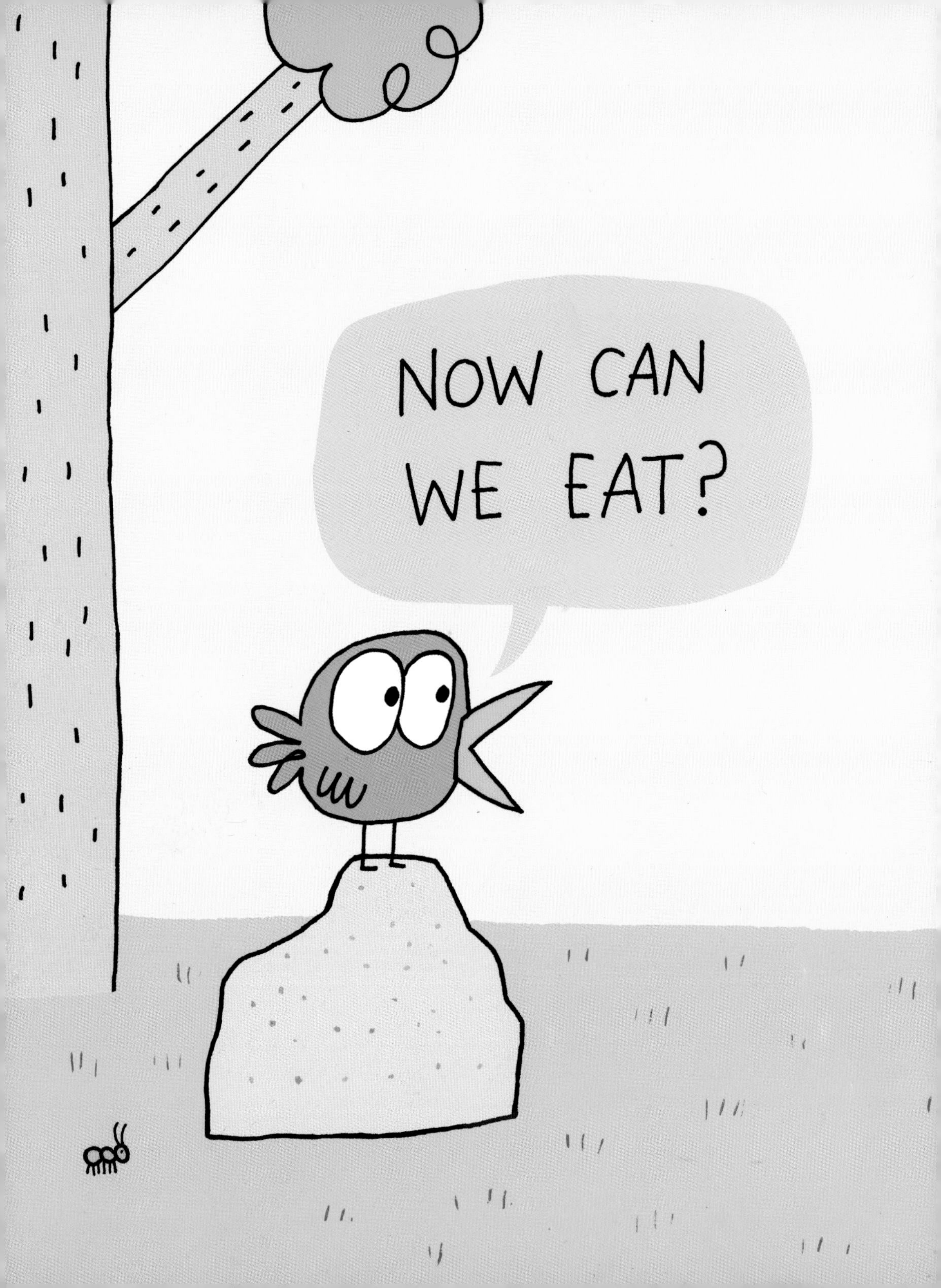
NOW CAN WE EAT?

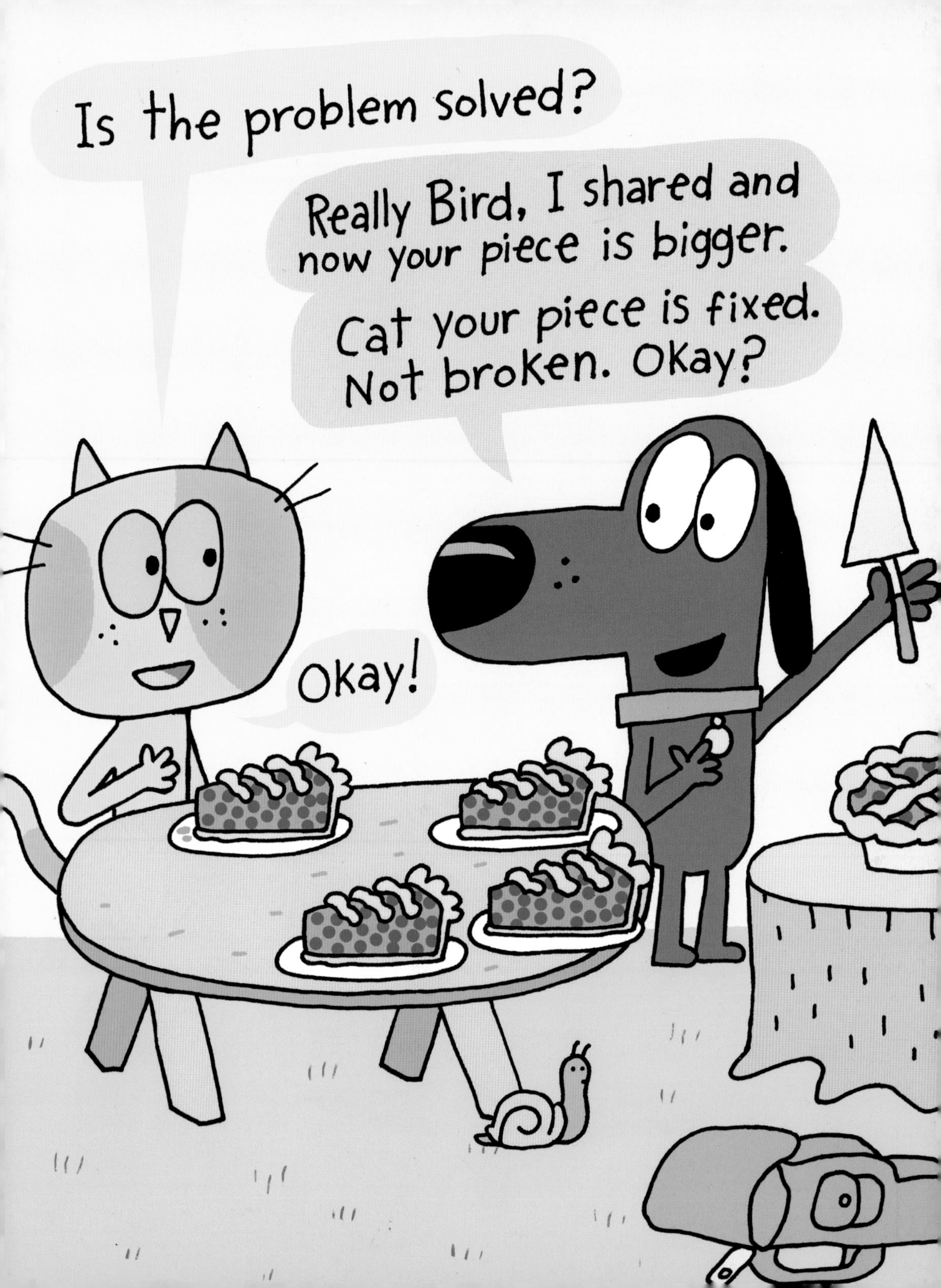
Is the problem solved?
Really Bird, I shared and now your piece is bigger.
Cat your piece is fixed. Not broken. Okay?
Okay!

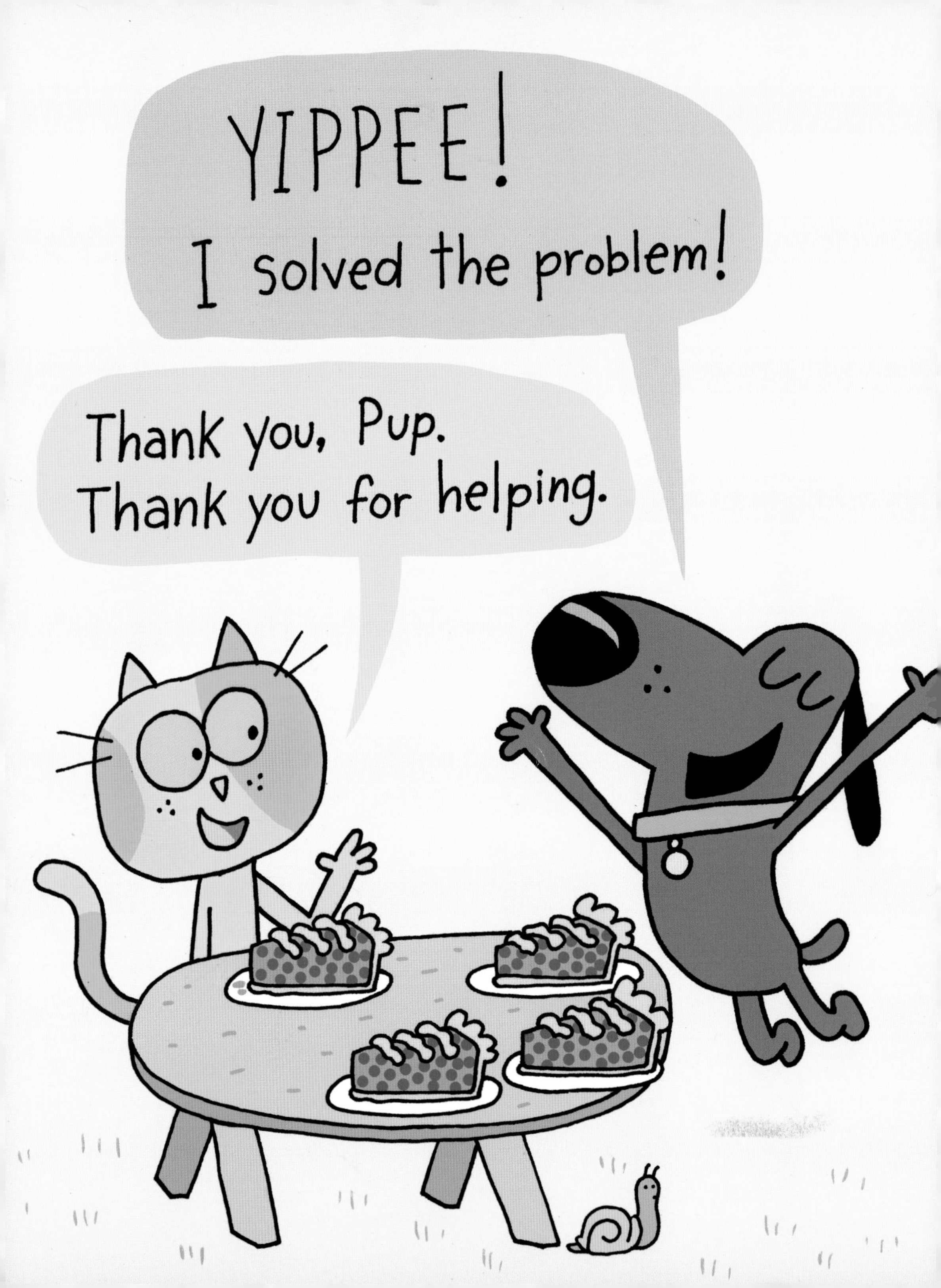
YIPPEE!
I solved the problem!
Thank you, Pup.
Thank you for helping.

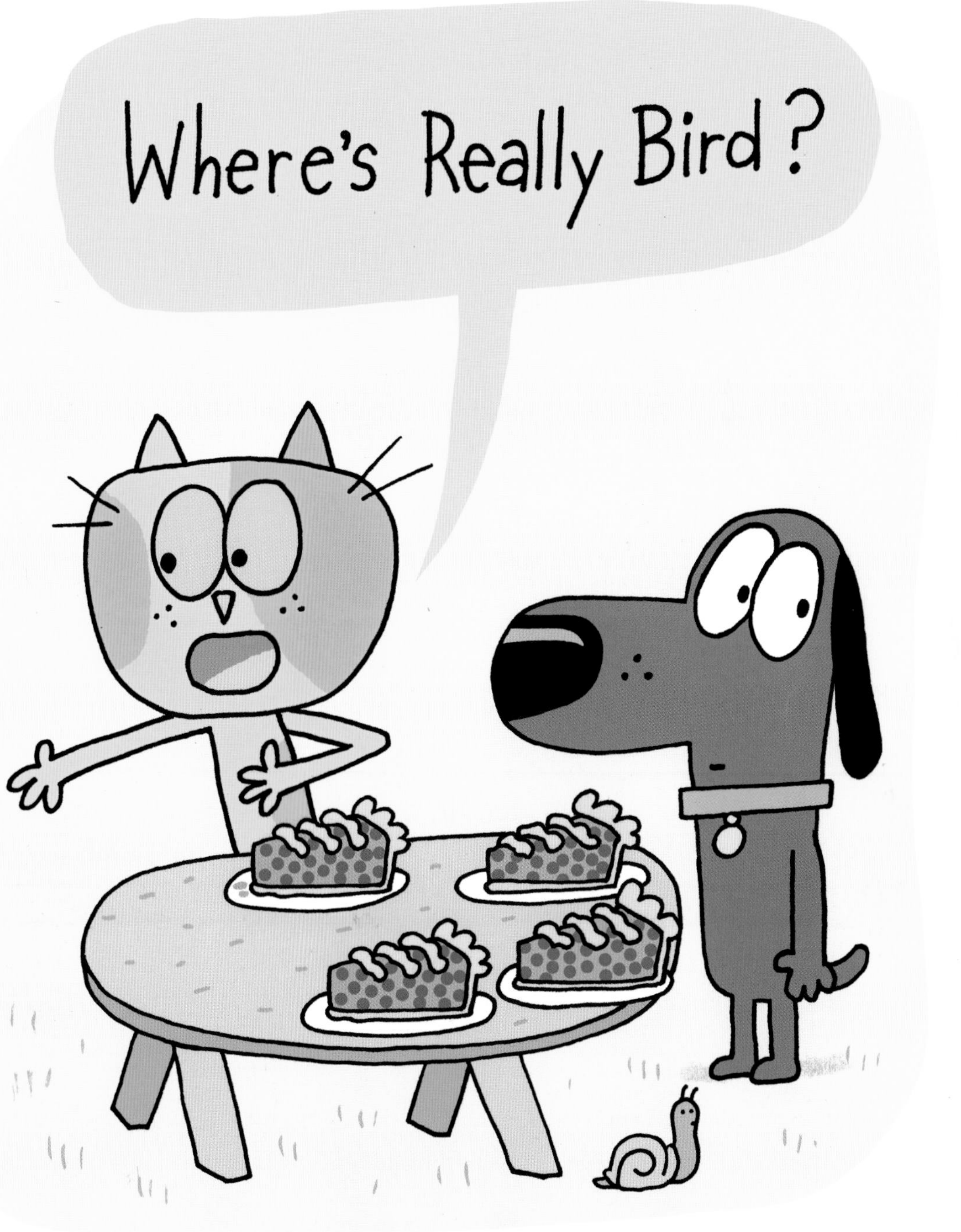
Where's Really Bird?

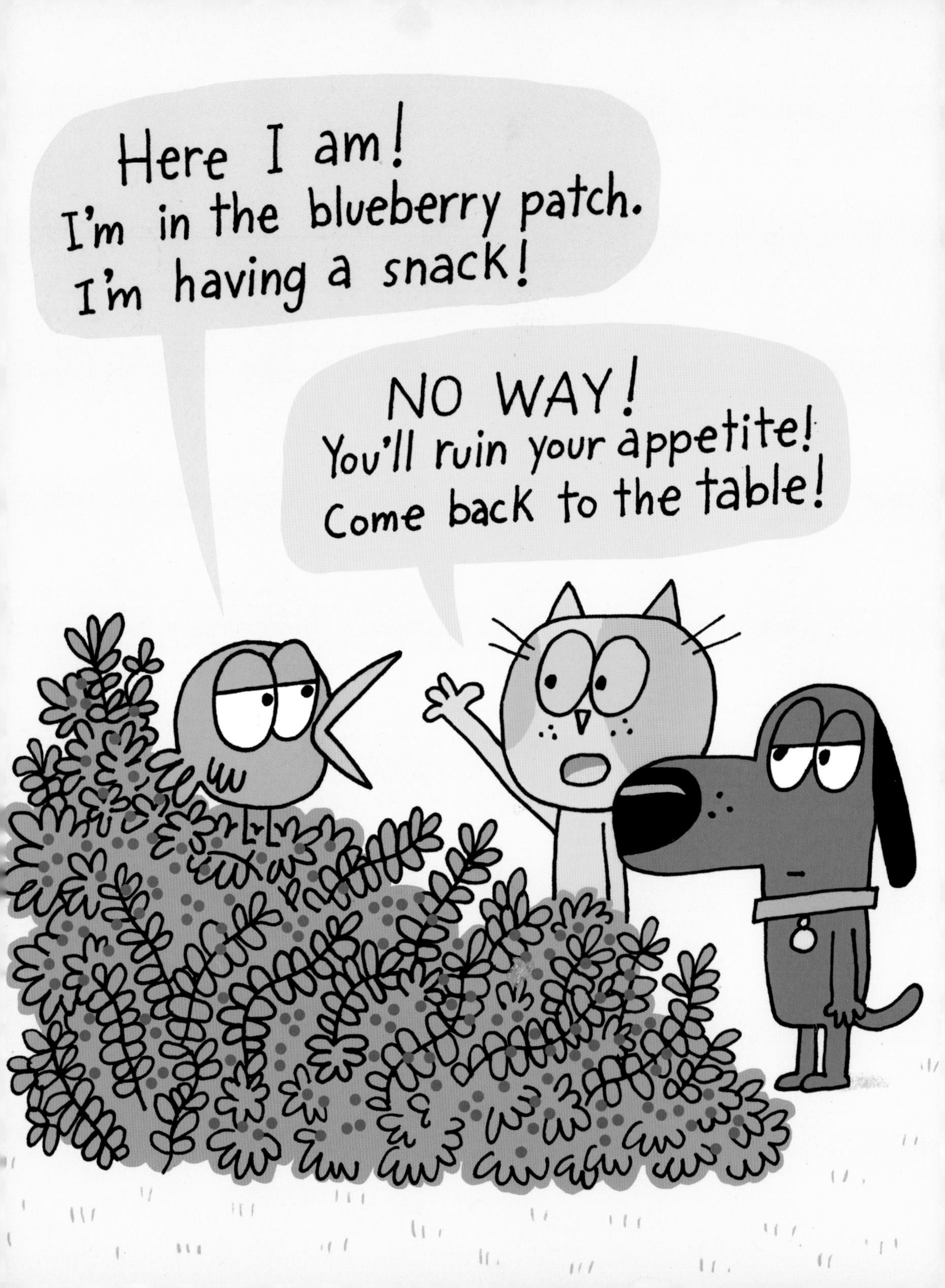
Here I am! I'm in the blueberry patch. I'm having a snack!
NO WAY! You'll ruin your appetite! Come back to the table!

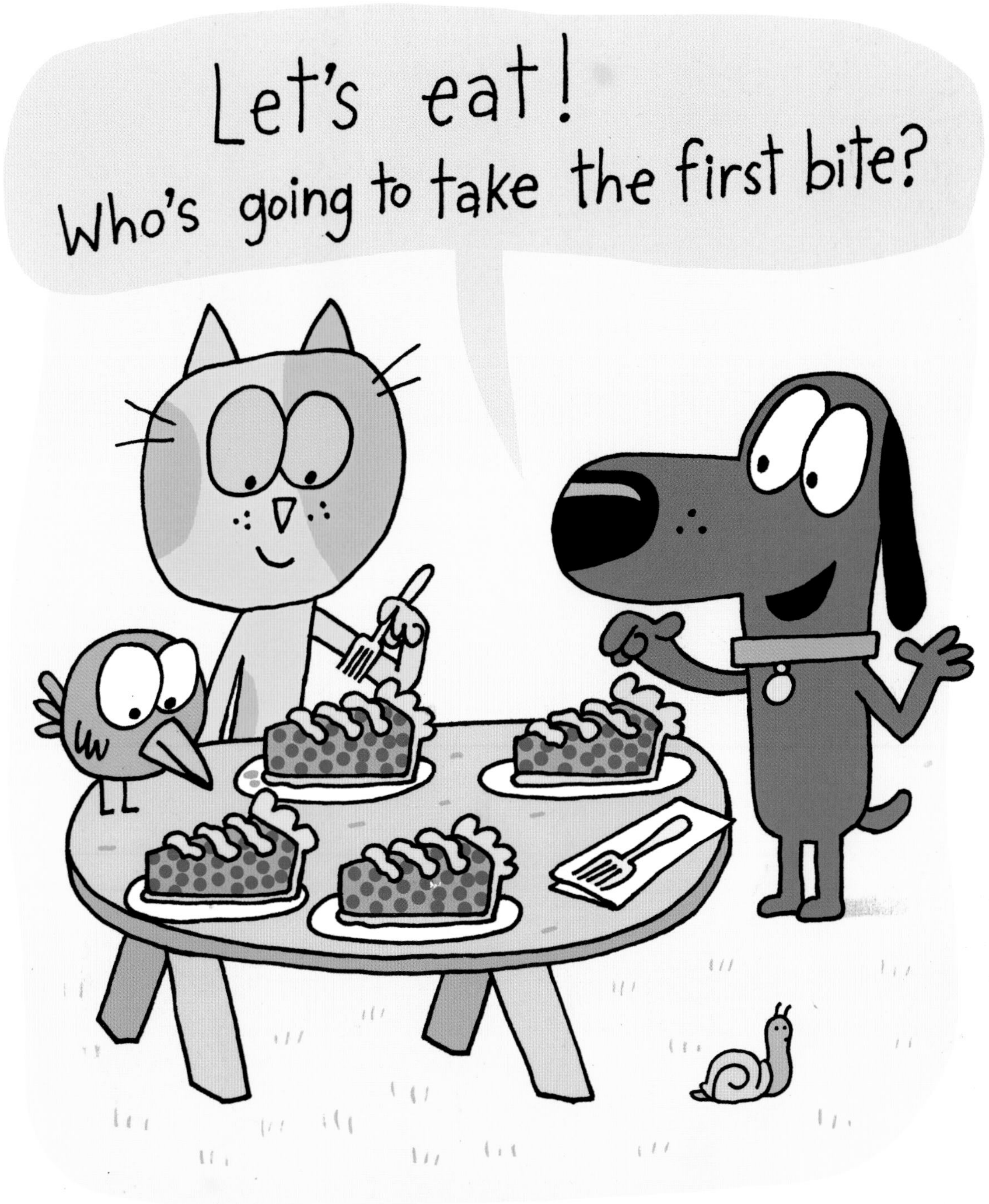
Let's eat!
Who's going to take the first bite?

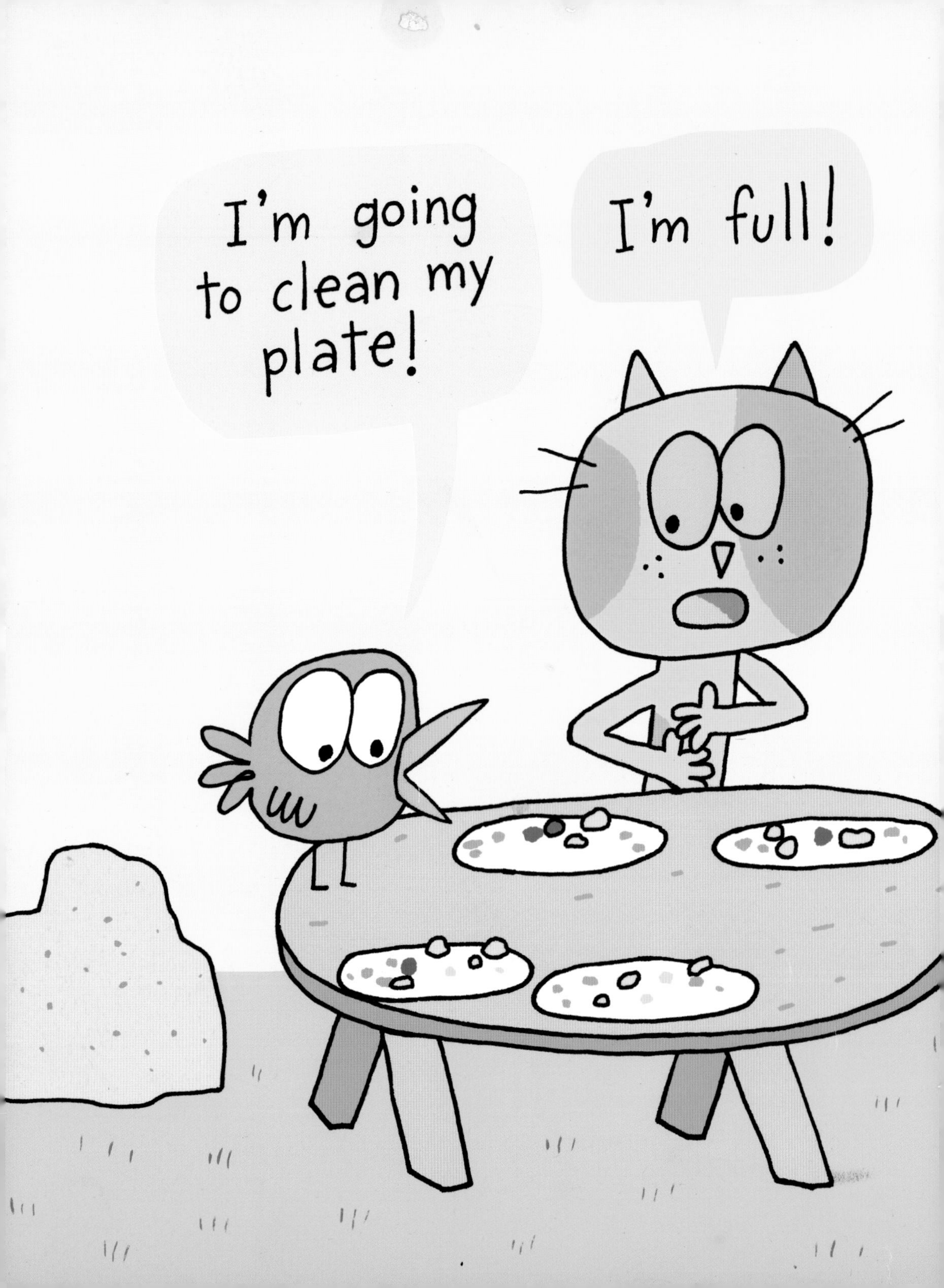
I'm going to clean my plate!
I'm full!

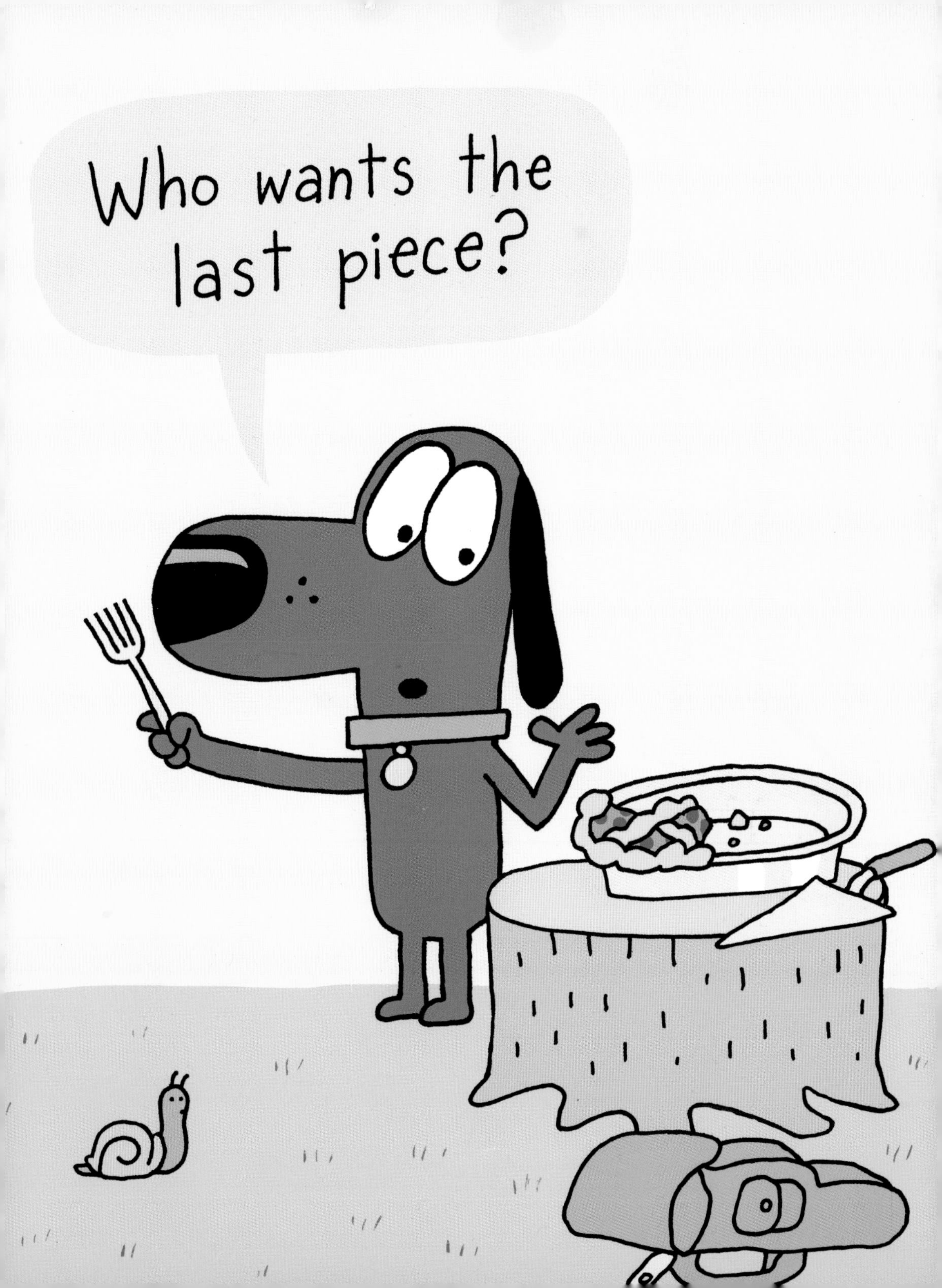
Who wants the last piece?

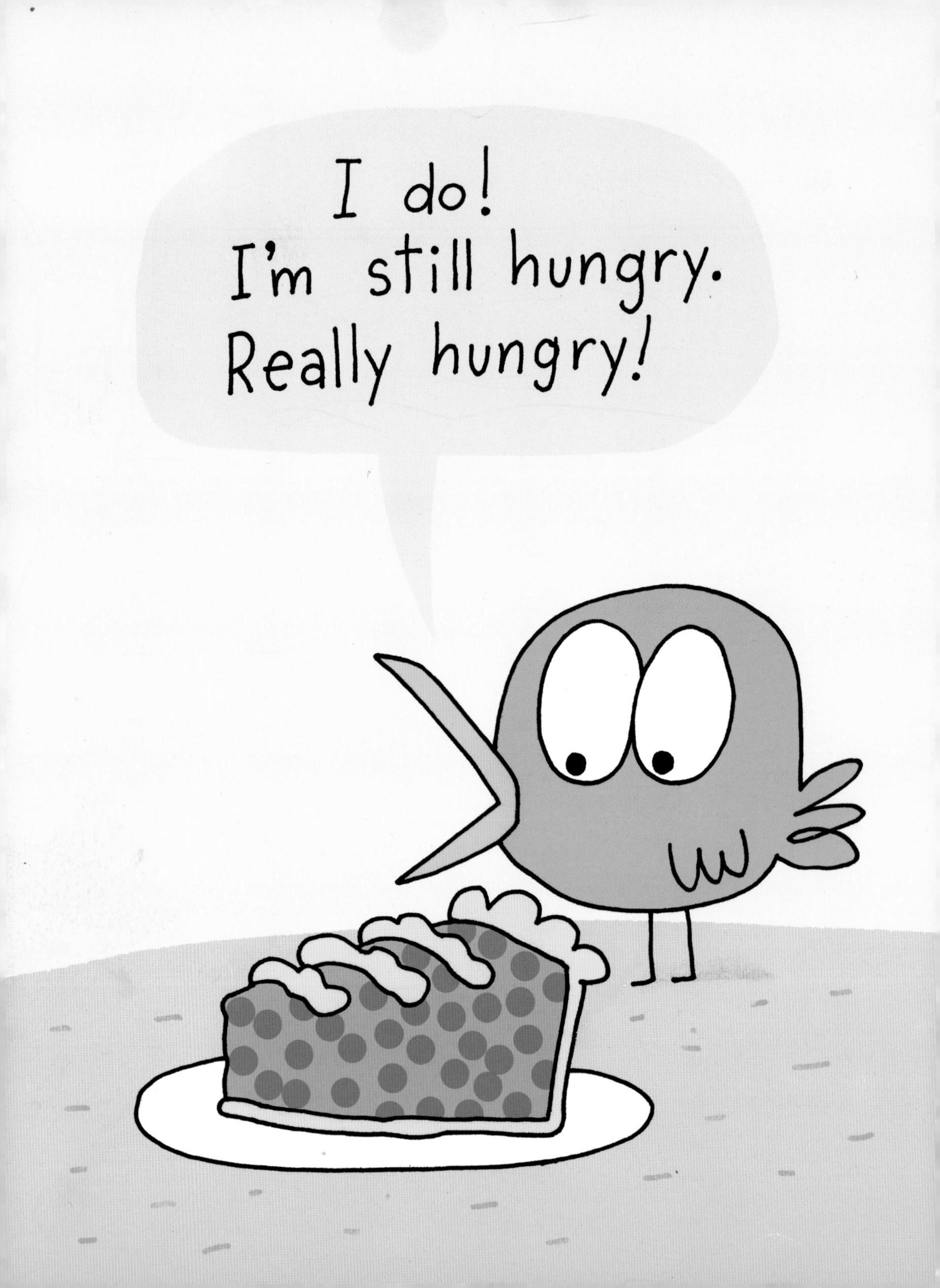
I do!
I'm still hungry.
Really hungry!

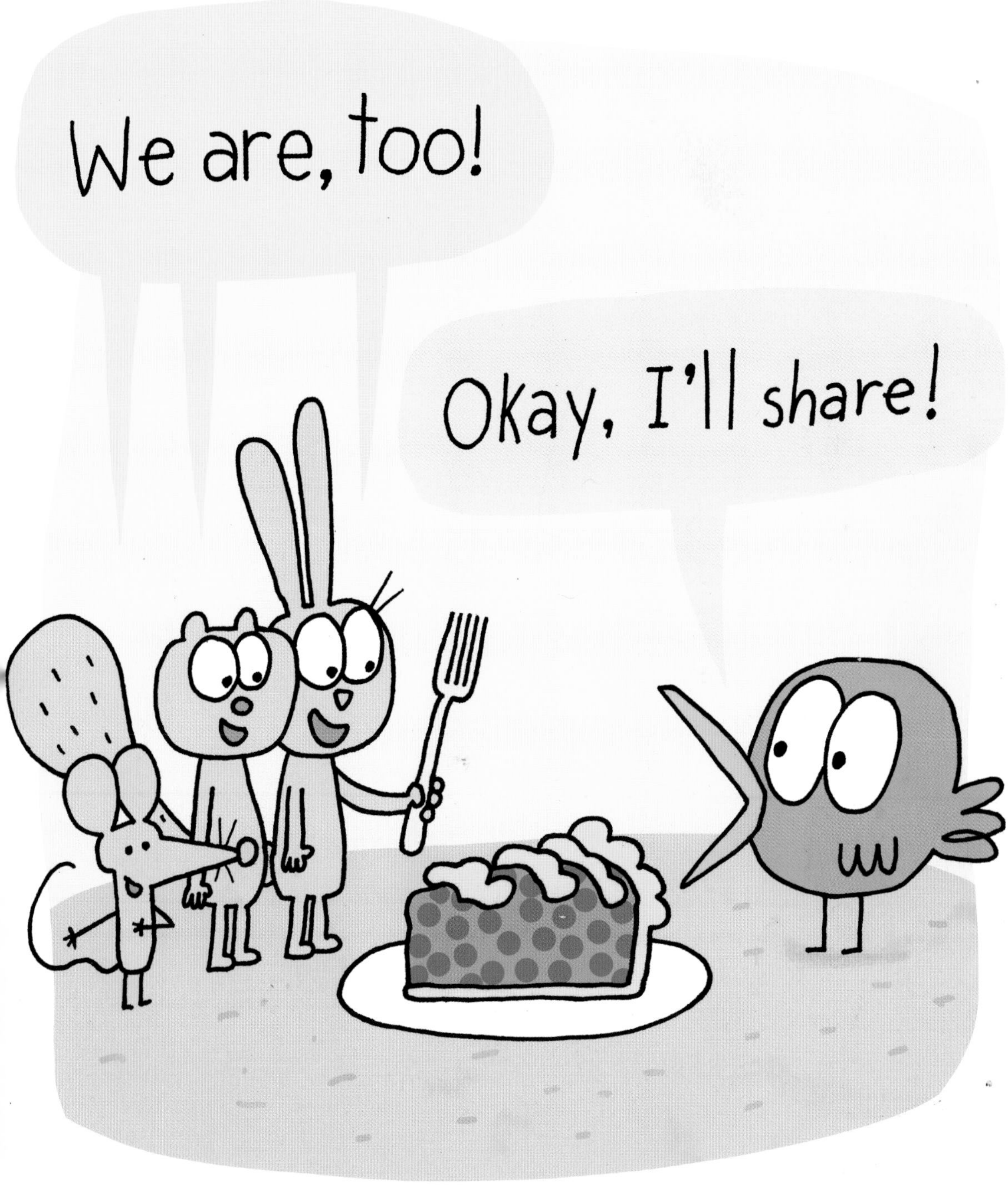
We are, too!
Okay, I'll share!

Think About / Talk About:

- Have you ever asked for a bigger piece?
  Of what?
  Did you eat it all up?

- What happens if your piece of pie is broken?
  Or if some of it is left in the pan?

- Did you ever have an argument about
  whose piece of pie, or cake, is better?
  What happened?
  Who solved the problem?
  Did a grown-up help?

- Draw a piece of pie just the way you like it.
  A purr-fect (perfect) piece!